MW01098431

I ESCAPED THE GRIZZLY MAZE

I ESCAPED
BOOK 13

ELLIE CROWE

SCOTT PETERS

If you purchased this book without a cover, you should be aware this is stolen property. It was reported as "stripped and destroyed" to the publisher, and neither the author nor the publisher has received any payment for this "stripped book."

I Escaped The Grizzly Maze (I Escaped #13)

Copyright © 2022 by Ellie Crowe and Scott Peters

All rights reserved.

No part of this book may be reproduced in any form or by any electronic or mechanical means, including information storage and retrieval systems, without written permission from the author, except for the use of brief quotations in a book review.

ISBN: 978-1-951019-37-2 (Hardcover)

ISBN: 978-1-951019-36-5 (Paperback)

While inspired by real events, this is a work of fiction and does not claim to be historically accurate or portray factual events or relationships. References to historical events, real persons, business establishments, and real places are used fictitiously and may not be factually accurate but rather fictionalized by the author.

Cover design by Susan Wyshynski

Best Day Books For Young Readers

ONE

THE GRIZZLY MAZE
KATMAI PENINSULA, ALASKA
OCTOBER 2003

Fifteen-year-old Cody shivered. Yikes, this place was cold. Out in the howling night, the wind shrieked and rain poured down. He wrapped his arms tighter around his chest and tried to catch some sleep.

Something rustled. Like a jack-in-the-box, Cody sat up. "What was that?"

A few feet away, his cousin Samantha tensed. "Don't know."

Then, like something out of a nightmare, the tent shuddered and a monster-sized head burst through the tent flap. Black eyes. Giant bear snout. Long teeth. Steaming breath reeking of fish and blood.

Terrified, Cody shouted. "Get away! Go! Get lost!"

Time stood still.

The grizzly watched him. Eyes cold. Focused. Strings of saliva dripped from its powerful jaws.

"Get out!" Samantha shrieked. "Get *out!*"

Her screams worked. The monster head disappeared.

"Whoa," Samantha breathed.

"Stay still," Cody hissed.

"I think it's gone," Samantha whispered. "I almost had a heart attack."

"Me too." Cody let out a nervous snort. "That was crazy. Too bad you didn't get a photo."

Without warning, a massive paw smashed through the flap.

TWO

Cody studied the grizzly posters in the Waldorf School corridor. "That documentary was so cool. Check out the size of those bears!"

"Yeah." Fifteen-year-old Samantha's blond ponytail bobbed as she nodded. "Massive! Amazing how that guy, Timothy Treadwell, isn't scared of them. Did you see how they followed him like big, furry dogs?"

"Can you imagine?" Cody eyed the bears' sharp teeth and claws. "But like he said, if he showed any weakness, they'd tear him to pieces."

"Aw," Samantha said. "They didn't look dangerous. He was right up close to them."

"Ha, you wouldn't say that if you got lost in that place

he called the grizzly maze. What if a humongous bear came barreling down a tunnel right at you?

Samantha said, "First, I'd take a picture. Then, I'd scream."

Cody laughed. "Treadwell is living with the bears again this fall. It would be cool if we could visit Gramps' cabin in Kodiak. Maybe we could check out the grizzly maze. We might even be able to talk to Treadwell. Get him to show us around, maybe he'll even let us see his bears."

"We'd never be allowed to miss school. And who's going to pay for it?"

Cody thought for a minute. "I have that money that my grandma left me. I bet Mom and Dad would let me spend it."

"All of your savings? Are you sure?"

"It would be a once-in-a-lifetime trip. And the science fair is coming up. We could do a project on protecting grizzlies. Treadwell is right—we should protect animals like that from poachers. We could visit the maze, interview him while we're there, and take pictures and everything. That would be a great project."

"We'd have to set it up with Tim Treadwell first, though, don't you think?"

"No, I mean, we can see the maze for ourselves. We can document how the place works. And then we'll drop into his camp. It has to be a pretty established place. I bet he'll be excited to see two students interested in his work. It will be even better if it's a surprise. He'll be super impressed."

"My mom and dad *are* into eco-warriors," Samantha said. "Treadwell definitely counts. They might go for it."

Cody said, "So, should we? Go for it?"

"Yes! Plus, I'll get to photograph native birds for my portfolio. And I bet Gramps would be up for visitors."

Cody grinned. "Alaska, here we come."

THREE

KODIAK ISLAND,
ALASKA
OCTOBER 2003

The Alaska Airlines plane circled over Kodiak airport and landed smoothly. Weary from the long flight from Los Angeles, Cody and Samantha grabbed their backpacks from baggage control.

They walked out into the terminal. Cody spotted a tall guy with flyaway blond hair at the Alaska Airlines ticket counter. The man wore jeans, sunglasses, a camo-print bandana, and a black leather jacket and was talking to the ticket agent.

"Look," Cody said. "Over there! That's got to be Tim Treadwell."

Samantha stared. "Wow! Is he just arriving, too? Talk about luck! Let's ask him for tips on the best places to see bears. Then we can casually mention we'd love to visit the grizzly maze—with him if possible."

"I like it. Stay cool, though," Cody said. "Not like a fangirl."

Samantha glared. "As if. You're the one fangirling."

"It's true," Cody said with a grin.

As they neared the ticket counter, the agent and Treadwell began arguing. Treadwell looked furious and the agent looked apologetic.

Treadwell's voice grew louder. "There's no way we're paying that. Highway robbery, that's what it is."

"I'm sorry, sir, if you want to leave Alaska today, that's the ticket price."

Treadwell was trying to leave? Cody was confused. He'd read that Treadwell was supposed to stay through the end of the month. What a bummer. They should have planned this better, not just assumed everything would work out. What had he been thinking?

Treadwell turned to the blond-haired woman at his side. Despite her high-heeled leather boots, she came to well below his shoulders.

"Come on, Amie," Treadwell said. "Let's get out of here. We'll go back to the maze and camp again. Ticket prices go down next week. We'll leave then." He grabbed his bags and headed for the exit.

The woman, Amie, grabbed her suitcase and backpack. She tucked her long hair behind her ears and hurried after him.

Cody was sorry for Treadwell having his plans ruined. Still, what a relief! They'd come all this way hoping to see him, and there he was. Cody shot Samantha an excited look and followed.

"In a way, it's good that we can't leave," Treadwell was saying. "Downy may be back at the maze. I'm worried about her. I haven't seen her all summer."

"I don't want to go back, Tim," Amie said. "It's too late in the season. There were a lot more bears, and those new alpha males were really aggressive."

"We'll be fine." Treadwell marched out of the terminal, looked up at the blue sky, and laughed. "The weather's glorious. No sign of winter. No need to worry. We'll grab our tents out of storage, pick up a week's supplies from Kodiak Sports, and get a floatplane out of here."

Cody was working up his courage to approach Treadwell when a mud-splattered jeep roared up, half-skidding out of control.

A familiar voice rang out. "Cody! Hey Cody! Come on. I can't park here, dude. Hurry up!"

Cody groaned. "What on earth is cousin Matt doing here?"

"No clue," Samantha muttered, sounding annoyed.

Their eighteen-year-old cousin had his usual wolverine look. Hairy. Greasy. Skinny arms covered in tattoos. At least instead of his usual scowl, Matt was grinning.

"Hey squirt, am I glad to see you," Matt called. "Gramps is on my case twenty-four-seven. It'll be good to have someone else he can pick on."

Cody winced. He hated being called squirt, and—cousin or not—he didn't like Matt. He had bad memories of Matt holding him upside down and shaking his lunch money and GI Joe out of his pockets. Cody hadn't enjoyed the head-in-the-toilet experience, either. Fortunately, he'd put on some muscle and grown a few inches. He'd be able to give as good as he got. But he still preferred to avoid Matt.

"I didn't know he'd be here," Samantha whispered as they headed toward the waiting jeep. "I guess Aunt Lucy is hoping Gramps can straighten him out. Did you hear he went joyriding in a neighbor's car and crashed into a streetlight?"

"Yep." Cody shot a frustrated glance toward Treadwell. The famous outdoorsman was hurrying toward a taxi. "Looks like we lost our chance to talk to him."

"We were so close!" Samantha said.

"Get a move on, dudes," Matt shouted.

Cody and Samantha climbed into the jeep.

Cody had an idea. "Hey Matt, you see that guy getting into the cab? That's Tim Treadwell."

"Okaaay?" Matt said. "Why should I care?"

"Just listen for a minute," Cody said. "He spent the last twelve summers living with grizzlies in Alaska. He's headed

9

to Kodiak Sports to stock up so he can go back and camp there. Samantha and I want to ask if he'll take us."

Matt raised his eyebrows. "Huh! You know what? I saw that guy on the Discovery Channel. He's famous. I bet I could make some money if I got pictures of him with those massive bears. That'll be way better than being at Gramps. I'll come with you."

Cody grimaced. *Over my dead body.* "Do you know where Kodiak Sports is?"

"Sure. And I know a shortcut." Matt revved the engine and took off down a gravel road. "This thing can do seventy on dirt."

A wide-eyed pedestrian leaped out of the way as Matt sideswiped a garbage can.

"Watch where you're going, sucker!" Matt yelled.

With a screech of brakes, he skidded into a sports store parking lot. A stuffed grizzly stood in the window. Inside, bear skins hung on the walls. A bear skull lamp glowed. At the counter, three hunters discussed ammunition.

There was no sign of Tim Treadwell.

Matt wandered over to study the guns. Cody and Samantha approached the balding store owner.

"What's the best place to see grizzlies around here?" Cody said.

"Not many bears around Kodiak now. There's been a drought—hardly any berries, nothing for the bears to eat. Most grizzlies have headed north to feed on salmon."

In a tight voice, Samantha said, "Are those men going to hunt bears?"

"Sure," the store owner said. "They're off into the back-country."

"That's awful." Samantha wrinkled her upturned nose. "Grizzlies should be protected."

The store owner stiffened. "You want to put me out of business?"

Sensing an argument, Cody stepped in. "Have you heard of the grizzly maze?"

The man nodded. "Yep."

"Do you have a map of the area?" Cody asked.

"Maps are over there. The grizzly maze is on the Katmai Peninsula."

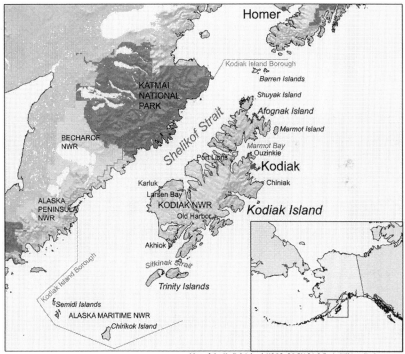

Map of the Kodiak Island, USGS, CC BY-SA 2.5, via Wikimedia Commons

The store owner turned to Samantha and, in a kinder voice, said, "Hunting's not allowed in Katmai National

Park. Besides, there are over thirty-thousand grizzlies up there, miss, so you don't need to fret about them."

"Thirty-thousand," Samantha said. "That's incredible."

"Certainly is."

Cody said, "What's the best bush pilot company to fly us up to the grizzly maze?" He'd researched a few but was curious to hear what the store owner had to say.

"They're all good. I don't recommend it, though, this late in the season. Place is dangerous right now. The bears are fattening up for their long winter hibernation and what with the drought, food is scarce."

"We know someone who goes there," Samantha said. "And he's going there now."

The store owner laughed. "Oh, I see. You met Tim Treadwell, did you?"

"Sort of," Cody said. "Do you know him?"

"Yep. But I doubt even Tim is going to the maze now." He chuckled, his rugged face crinkling. "Then again, I wouldn't put it past him. Tim is a great guy and he loves the grizzlies. But he believes they're his friends." His eyes darkened. "They're not."

A hunter who was listening in laughed. "Treadwell is just beggin' for trouble. Bears are wild animals, not friends. One wrong move and they'll tear you apart."

The store owner turned as the door opened. "Well, you're in luck, you can ask Treadwell all about it yourselves. Here he comes now."

FOUR

KODIAK ISLAND, ALASKA

Samantha's eyes widened as Tim Treadwell and his girlfriend breezed into the store. "They look like movie stars," she whispered.

The store owner rushed to greet the couple. "I thought you went home to Malibu for the winter, Tim."

Treadwell, tanned skin glowing from the cold, shook his head. "Didn't work out. We're flying up to the maze for another week."

"Bit late in the season, isn't it?"

"It's the toughest, most exciting month," Treadwell said. "Violent storms. Mobs of hungry bears."

The store owner looked worried. "Sounds dangerous."

"For some. Not me." Treadwell began filling a shopping basket with canned food. "The giant males are back at the maze. And lots of beautiful, sweet bears, too. I'm stopping poachers who shouldn't be hunting up there—my work is a success."

The store owner held up a spray can. "Need some bear spray?"

Cody noted the picture on the bear spray label—a ferocious grizzly poised to attack.

"Nah." Treadwell snorted. "Have you seen what that stuff does to bears? Why should they suffer for me?"

Amie touched Treadwell's arm. "We could get a few of those warning flares."

"Don't need them."

Amie said, "I'm scared of those big alphas that just arrived. We don't know them and they freak me out."

"Aw." Treadwell smiled down at her. "Those big males won't hurt you. They're just angry because they have no berries." He shook his fist at the roof. "God! Allah! We need more rain! Do you hear me? The bears are starving. Rain! We need it!"

Amie said, "This is the last time I'm going to the maze, Tim. I mean it."

Cody tried to think of something to say. This didn't seem the moment to talk to the eco-warrior.

Samantha nudged him.

Reluctantly, he stepped forward. "Um. Excuse me, sir, Mr. Treadwell. Could I talk to you for a moment?"

Treadwell turned. "Sure."

"My cousin and I saw the Discovery Channel documentary about you. It was great."

"Thanks," Treadwell said.

"We joined your group, the *Grizzly People*," Cody said. "We want to help protect grizzlies from illegal poachers."

"I appreciate it," Treadwell said. "Grizzlies are magnificent animals. Don't you think so, Amie?"

Amie gave a reluctant smile. "Tim says you haven't lived until you've bathed in a lake with grizzlies."

Cody grinned. "I sure haven't done that. But my cousin and I would love to go to the grizzly maze. Would that be possible, sir?"

"Sorry, guys. The grizzly maze is too dangerous for kids like you. Particularly now."

"Definitely too dangerous," Amie said. "Every bear in Katmai Peninsula is there."

"We'd stay out of your way," Cody said.

Matt chose that moment to show up. "We're not scared of grizzlies," he said. Then he laughed.

Treadwell eyed Matt up and down. "Not going to happen." He gathered up his purchases. As he and Amie went out the door, he waved at the store owner. "See you sometime in October if I don't perish."

Matt scowled and called out, "Poser!"

The door slammed.

Samantha rolled her eyes. "That helped."

"I don't care what that dude thinks," Matt said. "It's a free country. I'll go where I want. Hey, do either of you guys have credit cards?"

"Yeah, Dad authorized a credit card for me," Cody said. He didn't add that he'd be paying his dad back with his savings. "Why?"

"Duh! We need camping supplies."

"But Treadwell told us we can't go to the maze," Samantha said.

"He doesn't own the place," Matt said. "Now, start shopping. I'll get two pop-up tents; you grab sleeping bags and snacks and stuff. Enough for three days."

Samantha flashed Cody a worried look. "You're not seriously thinking of going up there, are you? After what Treadwell said?"

He sighed. "No. If he says it's a bad idea, I'm sure he's right. Bummer, though."

A hunter wandered over. "No need to go to the maze to see grizzlies. We got bears right here on Kodiak Island. Just head over to the Visitors Center—they'll give you directions where to camp."

"Great, thanks!" Cody said.

Camping would still be an adventure, even if they weren't with the world-famous bear expert. They'd make it work for the project.

If only Matt would lose interest now that they were staying in the area. Matt, though, got busy grabbing tents.

Cody filled his cart with a knife, matches, flashlight, cook pot, three sleeping bags, waterproof boots, fishing line, and a small ax. In the food aisle he added trail mix, granola bars, cans of Vienna sausages, sour-cream-and-onion Pringles, a water purifier, and a few bottles of water.

The bear spray was expensive. Cody studied the price, returned it to the shelf, then grabbed it again. Better safe than sorry.

He snuck a look at the stuffed grizzly in the store window. Wow, that was one huge bear. It stood nine feet high. Poor guy—doomed to stare out at a parking lot forever. In most places, grizzlies had been hunted to extinction. It was good to hear they were making a comeback in Katmai Park. But Treadwell said that illegal poachers were going after them. Cody's science project was worthwhile. He'd learn what he could in Kodiak and find a way to interview Treadwell by phone or email.

Nearby, Matt pulled the largest hunting rifle from the rack.

"We don't need that," Cody said. "I'm buying bear spray."

"You'll thank me later, kiddo," Matt said. "When I save your life."

Again, Cody hesitated. He was paying for all this stuff. Better safe than sorry.

The store owner rang up the supplies. "Remember, no one's allowed to camp near bears. In fact, even Katmai National Park has a new rule, a five-day limit at any camping spot. And tents must be kept at least a mile away from bears." He grinned. "Some rangers call it the Treadwell Rule."

"Why?" Samantha said.

"They reckon he bothers the bears."

"How could he bother the bears?" Cody said. "He's trying to protect them."

"You'd have to ask the rangers."

"I can't wait to see those grizzlies," Matt said. "The bigger, the better."

The store owner frowned. "Don't be like Treadwell. It's not a case of *if* something will happen to Tim. It's a case of *when*. He thinks they're his friends. Grizzlies aren't humans in bear costumes. Remember that."

FIVE

KODIAK ISLAND, ALASKA

Cody, Samantha, and Matt headed out of the store loaded down with gear. They jumped up into the jeep.

Samantha said, "How far is it to Gramps' cabin?"

"It's in the middle of nowhere," Matt said. "We'll call Gramps to say we're going camping, and we'll catch him in a couple of days."

"It's kind of late to find a campsite," Cody said, eyeing the darkening sky.

Matt snorted. "Who said we'd set up tonight? You've got a credit card. We'll check into the Best Western."

Cody made a quick calculation in his head. Now that he wasn't paying for flights up to the grizzly maze, he had money to spare. "Okay, we can do one night."

Samantha's eyes lit up. "Cool. Tomorrow, we'll go to the Visitors' Center and talk to a guide."

Hotel guests crammed the Kodiak Best Western's large

lobby. A huge bearskin covered the floor near the stone fire-place, and a bear skull hung on the wall. Hunters, anglers, and tourists, all bubbling and animated, filled the restaurant.

Excited to be in such an unusual place, Cody munched down fish and chips and watched boats bobbing on the dark blue marina. Samantha snapped photos of swooping seag-ulls. Matt was unusually quiet, staring out the large windows. Uneasy, Cody wondered what he was plotting.

Up in the hotel room, Matt claimed one of the two beds. Cody told Samantha to take the other one, and he called the front desk for a cot. Exhausted, he flopped onto it.

The sounds of screeching seagulls and grunting sea lions mingled with Matt's snores, and Cody fell asleep fast.

He woke to find Matt gone. Samantha ordered pancakes

from room service. Cody felt antsy. He wanted to get over to the Visitor's Center.

As he licked the last drop of maple syrup off his fork, Matt stomped in, grinning.

"Get dressed, hurry, we leave in an hour." Matt waved tickets at them. "We're going to the grizzly maze."

Cody stared. "You talked to Tim Treadwell? He's taking us?"

"Nope. We have our own ride. A floatplane. The flight to Katmai Peninsula leaves in thirty minutes."

Samantha pushed her bangs out of her eyes. "Wow! How are we doing that?"

"Easy. I got the front desk to book the flights." Matt handed a credit card to Cody. "Here's your card. I borrowed it."

Cody stared. "I never said you could use my credit card. That's more than my savings, and Dad said I could only go over it for emergencies."

Matt laughed. "Seemed like an emergency to me. Get a move on. I've got this whole thing under control!"

Cody grabbed the tickets. Matt had gotten the worst deal possible. "I can't do that. These cost a fortune. I have to check with my dad."

"No point," Matt said. "No refunds on the tickets. Get a move on. This is going to be a blast."

Samantha said, "But it's not safe."

"Don't be a baby," Matt said. "We're only going for one night. And if it gets sketchy, I'll call the pilot to pick us up. Now let's go!"

SIX

KATMAI NATIONAL PARK

The floatplane's engine built from a low grumble to a steady thud. Cody zipped up his windbreaker and fastened his seatbelt.

He tried to swallow his guilt and resentment and focused on being excited instead. They were actually going to Katmai National Park! He'd work as a lifeguard next summer to repay Mom and Dad.

The plane roared into the cloudy sky and the marina dropped away. Below, the ocean glittered like rippled steel. Wind whipped at the surface and a pod of whales emerged from the white caps.

"Storm's moving in," the pilot shouted over the engine noise. "Hang on, it's going to be a bumpy ride."

The small plane shuddered, and Cody held tight to the armrests. A violent gust tossed the seaplane upward. His stomach lurched.

"That's Katmai Peninsula," the pilot shouted.

Below lay boggy tidal flats and dark forests. Snow blanketed the jagged mountain peaks, and Cody spotted two blue lakes enclosed by high mountains. A river connected them, and the nearest lake emptied into the ocean through a narrow gap.

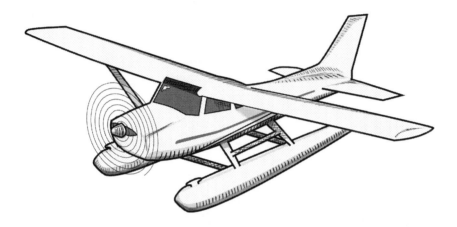

The pilot circled and descended. "Kaflia Lake," she said. "There are two lakes, an upper and a lower. I'll set us down in the ocean near the mouth of the lower lake."

Cody turned to Matt. "We don't know which lake Treadwell camps at."

Matt shrugged. "Who cares? We don't need Treadwell."

As the plane descended, Cody grabbed his binoculars and searched for Treadwell's camp without luck.

Below, dark slivers of spawning salmon leaped through the waves. He gaped when he saw a massive grizzly grabbing for fish with its claws. Then he saw another and another. Whoa. This place was unreal.

With a hissing thrum, the floatplane landed well clear of

the bears. They taxied through the shallow water to the shore.

The pilot stood up and took off her headphones. "Everybody okay?"

"Yes!" Samantha beamed. "That was amazing!"

"No." Matt hurled all over Samantha's new boots.

The smell was horrible.

With a stoic expression, Samantha cleaned up with a bottle of water and some napkins.

"Not my fault," Matt said and glared at the pilot.

"So, you're camping with Tim Treadwell for a few days?" the pilot asked.

"Yeah," Matt said.

The pilot squinted at the creek around a mile away. "There're a lot of grizzlies over there. I don't like leaving you kids. What time is Treadwell meeting you?"

"Well, he's not—" Cody began.

"He's on his way," Matt interrupted. "We'll be fine. We've been here before. Lots of times."

Cody gaped at Matt. *Liar!*

"Okay." The pilot gave Matt a satellite phone. "This is included in our flight package—call us if there's an emergency. Just a heads up, though, sat phones are expensive. You break it, you pay for it. And stay away from that grizzly-packed creek."

"We will, thanks," Cody said. He focused his binoculars on the massive animals. His heart beat faster. Those guys were as big as Buicks. "What do you guess those grizzlies weigh?"

"More than a thousand pounds," the pilot said. "You'll only spot enormous ones like that out here in Katmai. Like I said, steer clear. There are some new aggressive alpha males

24

in the pack. They're all fattening up for winter. Don't draw their attention."

Wide-eyed, Samantha swallowed hard.

"Thanks for the warning," Cody said. "Where are the park rangers?"

"There're no rangers here now," the pilot said. "The park advises tourists not to come when the bears are fattening up. I'm not sure why Treadwell invited you. If he doesn't turn up by four, call me and I'll come back for you."

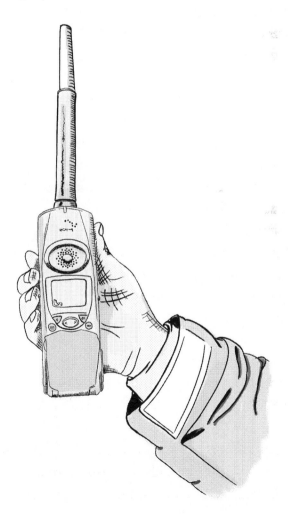

"Thanks. We'll contact you if we don't find Treadwell," Cody said, and he meant it.

"Right," the pilot said. "I'll be listening for your call." She climbed into the cockpit and slammed the door.

Matt muttered, "We know what we're doing and I have a rifle."

They waded to shore through the icy water. Cody was glad he'd bought rain boots, though they felt a size too big. He kept a wary eye on the grizzlies, even though they were a mile away.

Over there, tangled brambles and alder trees with skeletal, spiky branches stretched away from the lakeshore. That must be the gnarled woods known as the grizzly maze. How had Treadwell described it? As a labyrinth of tunnels made by bears.

Now that Cody saw it for real, it wasn't like some nature movie. It was scary and he couldn't believe Treadwell wandered around in there.

"Let's pitch the tents," Matt said.

"Not till Treadwell's plane lands," Cody replied. "Otherwise, we're leaving at four. I'm surprised he's not here yet."

"Coward," Matt muttered.

"Let's eat something. Then I want to take notes and make some sketches for the project," Cody said.

"Sound good," Samantha agreed. "I'll unpack my zoom lens. I should be able to get some great photos."

Sitting on his bag, Cody crunched Pringles. He could smell the sour cream and onion on his fingers. Would it attract bears? He rubbed his smelly hands with wet sand.

He studied the grizzlies through his binoculars. They

hadn't come closer and weren't looking this way. Still, they were fast—with a powerful sense of smell.

He shoved the empty Pringles can into his backpack. "No food lying around, okay?"

Matt laughed. "Chill out, will you?"

Cody said, "Hey, grizzlies killed two girls in Glacier National Park because tourists left garbage around, and the bears smelled it."

Matt laughed. "You worry too much."

"It's not worry, it's common sense. They're wild animals, and this is their habitat. We're just visitors, and we have to respect that."

"Blah blah blah," Matt said.

"Really? What would you do if a grizzly came right at us?" Cody said.

"I'd run," Samantha said.

"Running is the worst thing to do," Cody said. "A grizzly can run forty miles an hour. That's like a car."

Samantha shot him a mischievous smile. "Yeah. But I'd only have to run faster than you."

Cody rolled his eyes, laughing. "Great, I'll keep that in mind."

Then he took out his notebook, she set up her camera, and they both got to work.

SEVEN

KATMAI NATIONAL PARK

An hour later, the grizzlies were still foraging in the creek.

"The tide's going out," Cody said. "I want to check out the sea floor. Anyone coming?"

"In a minute." Samantha had her eyes glued to the white trumpeter swans cruising the lake. "Ooh, look! That swan's taking off. Check out the wings. Those must be five feet across."

"Later." Matt yawned.

"If you're going down to the ocean, take the rifle," Samantha said.

Matt got to his feet. "No way. It's my rifle." He lunged, putting Cody in a fake-friendly headlock.

Cody stepped hard on Matt's foot. He'd grown six inches since he'd last seen his cousin. *Not so easy to headlock me now, huh?*

"I don't want the rifle," Cody said.

Notebook in one hand and ax in the other, Cody hiked down the sloping dunes. The low tide had exposed miles of rippling sea floor. Tiny pools of water glistened, caught between the rocks. They brimmed with sea creatures. He stomped through a patch of seagrass, rounded a massive wet boulder, and gasped.

A cream-colored mother bear with two cubs rummaged in the sand, scooping up clams.

Cody backed away and ducked behind the boulder, heart pounding, then took a careful peek.

Incredible!

He knew mother bears were dangerous and that he should leave. But the bear was beautiful, and the roly-poly cubs were so cute—balls of wiggly fur, tumbling, wrestling, and munching on clams. He crouched lower and did a rough sketch, making notes in the margin.

- *mother bear has good coat but thin overall*
- *both cubs stay close, one copies mother bear's digging*
- *mother sniffs sand to locate more clams, she clearly smells them through the dirt*
- *she crushes whole clam in her mouth and spits out the shell, like eating sunflower seeds!*

A red fox darted between the mother bear's legs and grabbed a clam. Cody muffled a surprised laugh at the gutsy fox.

Wait till everyone at school hears about this.

Matt might have acted like a jerk, but Cody was suddenly glad they'd come. No wonder Treadwell loved this place. The grizzlies were unreal; no wonder he wanted to protect them.

A thrumming sound broke the silence. A floatplane leveled and descended, coming to a halt in the ocean shallows.

Awesome! Treadwell was here, everything was going to work out. Cody stowed his notebook and prepared to wave his arms.

But it wasn't Treadwell. Instead, two bearded men in canvas jackets and waterproof pants climbed out onto the floats. Both men held shotguns.

Poachers!

The mother grizzly reared up. Muscles rippling, eyes narrowed, it focused on the poachers.

Horrified, Cody watched as a poacher aimed and fired.

The grizzly reeled sideways. Then the mother and cubs loped away. If only he'd taken the rifle, he could fire it into the air and scare off the men.

Instead, all he could do was wave his ax wildly. "That's illegal! Get away from here!"

The poacher whirled around. "What the heck? Mind your own business, kid!"

"I just contacted the rangers," Cody yelled. "They're on their way."

The poachers scowled.

Meanwhile, the bears had disappeared.

The poachers shook their heads and climbed back into the floatplane. Cody sighed in relief as it rose into the sky.

A hundred feet away, the cubs darted out of the seagrass, shaking like frightened puppies. Eyes confused, they wandered toward Cody, wailing. Where was the mother bear? Had she been injured? He crouched and dug up a clam, stomped on it, and heard the satisfying crack of a shell.

He tossed the clam to the cubs. "Here you are, little guys."

Too late, he remembered you weren't supposed to feed wild animals.

A dark shape rose from the seagrass. Oops. The mother bear was right there. Cody dropped down fast. He didn't dare move. Shivering, he lay flat for what seemed ages. Finally, the mother bear went back to sniffing and digging for clams.

Something prodded his boot. Muscles spring-loaded, he turned.

The fox was trying to get its teeth into the sole that had smashed the clam. Smiling, Cody moved his foot and the fox darted away.

A faint, cracking sound echoed from the distant surf. A massive bear was feasting on the beached carcass of a killer whale. Yikes. Paws holding the skull, the grizzly gnawed into it fast and hard.

If that bear got hold of me, it could bite through my leg bone like a toothpick. Good thing it's far away.

Still, he was spooked and crept away fast. He was nearing dry sand when he heard a scream.

"Bear!" Matt's voice was shrill.

Before Cody could work out what was happening, Matt charged down the dunes right at him. A brown grizzly with a powerfully muscled body followed at a gallop.

Face frantic, breathing hard, Matt raced right by Cody, heading toward the sea.

The grizzly slowed.

Keen, dark eyes focused on Cody.

Cody stepped back. One of his too-large boots caught on a rock and he stumbled. Down he went, on to his knee. His mind seized up.

I'm going to die.

"Help!" Matt screamed. "Help!"

The grizzly pivoted and zoned in on Matt.

This is my chance. Blind with fear, Cody ran in the opposite direction.

Matt shrieked. "Help me! Cody, help me!"

Cody slowed. All he wanted to do was keep running. Why should he risk his life to save that jerk?

"Help, Cody! Help!" Matt slipped and landed on his butt with a splash.

Cody gritted his teeth and forced himself to shout and wave the ax. The bear turned halfway between the cousins.

We're going to be ripped to shreds.

The grizzly held its ground.

Cody stomped hard. "Get! You get!"

It was two against one. But the odds were still in favor of the grizzly.

"Get! Now!" Cody shouted, spinning the ax. Treadwell's words in the documentary pounded in his brain. *Make the bear believe you are more powerful than he is.*

They faced off—Cody wielding the ax round and round, yelling in a deep voice, the bear moving forward with fake charges and then retreating.

Just don't trip on another rock, whatever you do. Remember your flipping boots are too big. Do not trip!

Cody shouted again, his throat hoarse. To his utter amazement, the bear turned and loped off.

"I guess that one was a vegetarian." Cody's voice shook so hard he could barely speak. "What were you doing? You almost got us killed."

"Relax, dude. Don't be a drama queen." Matt talked big, but he was pale with shock.

"I'm calling that pilot for a ride out. Right now," Cody said.

"Whatever." Matt got to his feet, his pants dripping wet.

Cody held out his hand. "Where's the sat phone?"

"I have it." Hands shaking, Matt fiddled with the thing. He scowled. "Piece of junk. There's no reception."

"It worked at the tent," Cody said.

Trembling, Matt stumbled through the waves toward shore, holding the sat phone high. "Hello, hello, come in, come in," he yelled, hands shaking. "Hello. Hello. Anyone there?"

Matt collided with a rock and lost his footing.

Cody grabbed Matt's jacket.

Matt reached for Cody to steady himself.

And dropped the sat phone into the sea.

EIGHT

KATMAI NATIONAL PARK

Cody dove for the sat phone. He dried it on his shirt and shook it. "Dead."

"No problem," Matt said. "It'll work again if we bury it in sand."

"Sand! Give me a break."

"Sure, it will. I dropped my phone in the toilet and I put it in rice, and it worked."

"Sand won't work."

"This is all your fault," Matt said. "If you hadn't tripped and grabbed my jacket, I never would have dropped the sat phone."

"I didn't grab your jacket because I tripped. I was trying to save you."

"Dude, you know you totally made me fall," Matt yelled. "You can't even run in those dumb rain boots."

"Cody!" Samantha shouted, running across the sand.

"Matt!" She hugged them both. "That was close. Call the pilot. I don't want to stay here another minute."

"The sat phone's fried," Cody said.

"Fried? It can't be. Let me see." Samantha shook the sat phone and rubbed it with her sweater. "Oh no. How are we going to get back? The pilot will think we're with Tim Treadwell. We're stuck."

Cody said, "We have to find Treadwell. He must have landed before we got here."

"We would have seen him," Samantha said.

"Maybe he's at the upper lake. He must be."

"Maybe."

Cody said, "We'll go there and get help."

Eager, Samantha nodded. "We'll be safe with him. He knows what he's doing."

Matt snorted. "Give me a break. You have to hike through those grizzly tunnels to get there. No way am I doing that."

"Well, Cody and I are going." Samantha's voice had turned to steel. Once she put her mind to something, she stuck to it.

"Good luck!" Matt said with a sneer.

"Thanks," she said. "Because unless we get a ride back to Kodiak, we're spending the winter here. In case you forgot, we didn't tell Gramps or anyone else where we were going."

Matt paled as the weight of her words sank in. To Cody's shock, he seemed about to cry.

"We never should have come," Matt said. "It's all your kids' fault."

Samantha's face turned red with indignation. "You bought the tickets!"

"I'm not walking through that maze. I'm staying here," Matt said. "Come get me when you find help."

Cody nodded. "Okay. When we find Treadwell, we'll use his sat phone to call our pilot to come get us. He must have one, don't you think? Just stay near the beach and keep an eye out."

"Whatever," Matt said. "Just hurry it up."

Samantha let out a yelp and took off toward their stuff. Cody's stomach dropped. What now?

Samantha charged across the dunes. "You little brat!"

Too late. The red fox had found their supplies. In dismay, Cody took in the mess. The trail mix packets were torn, raisins and nuts scattered. The energy bars were half-chewed. The only things left intact were cans and bottles. A strange smell covered everything.

Samantha looked close to tears. "Now we've hardly anything to eat. What if we don't find Treadwell?"

"You can't leave me here with no food," Matt said. "We'll have to catch a fish first."

"Catch one yourself." Cody was furious. "We have to get through the grizzly maze before dark." He walked around, trying to salvage some food. Everything smelled like fox pee.

He opened the sports store map. "Good thing the fox didn't pee on this." A thin blue line showed a creek leading from the lower to the upper lake. Using the scale and his fingers, he tried to estimate the distance. "It's about a mile. We should go."

Matt grabbed the rifle and the energy bars. "I'll keep these."

The three glared at one another.

Cody backed down first. What was the point? Matt wasn't going to change. He picked up the ax and Samantha took half the fishing line and hooks. Hopefully, this wouldn't take long.

"Take care, Matt," Cody said. "You sure you want to stay by yourself?"

Matt nodded. "Yep."

"Then we'll see you soon," Cody said, picturing the dark, ominous tunnels that awaited them.

Samantha grimaced, uncertain. "Hopefully."

NINE

KATMAI NATIONAL PARK
THE GRIZZLY MAZE

Cody led the way around the lower lake, wading in knee-deep water. Small birds and dragonflies fluttered in the reeds.

"Awesome!" Samantha whipped out her camera. "Wait a sec."

"Hurry up, Ansel Adams," Cody said. "This water's cold."

He slipped a few times and barely managed to keep his balance. Tonight would be freezing, worse if he got soaked. Hypothermia was a real danger.

Samantha said, "It would be easier if we walked on the shore."

"Where? The brambles reach the water."

They moved as fast as possible, keeping an eye out for danger until they'd reached the rambling mess of brush and spiky alders. Here and there, narrow tunnels burrowed away into the gloom.

Puffing, Cody said, "The grizzly maze. This must be it."

"There sure are a lot of tunnels." Samantha glanced left and right, her shoulders up around her ears. "I wonder where the bears went?"

"I don't know," Cody said, lowering his voice. "Let's just count our luck and get going."

"I wonder which tunnel goes to the upper lake?"

"This one's wider." Cody edged into a snaking tunnel. "This place would be seriously cool if I wasn't so freaked out. Check out these bear prints," he whispered and put his foot into one of them. He wore size eleven shoes, but the print dwarfed his foot.

"Shh," Samantha warned. "Just walk."

The maze was creepy. A dark labyrinth, low and claustrophobic. In sections, Cody ducked to keep his baseball cap from catching in the brambles. Samantha kept stepping on his heels.

"It stinks like poop," she whispered.

"I know."

"What if a grizzly shows up?"

"Fall down and play dead. Don't think about it."

Samantha said nothing.

The tangled branches grew thicker until he had to squint to see. All around was stifling, clingy darkness.

A thought came to him. "In Glacier, Gramps had a hiking stick with a bell to warn bears."

"And?"

"Maybe we should warn the bears we're coming," he whispered. "Sing or something."

"Sing?" Samantha hissed. "I think we should be quiet."

"Gramps says bears don't want to meet humans any more than we want to meet them."

Samantha groaned. "I guess Gramps knows. Either that or you're going to get us killed." Quietly, she sang, "*If you go down to the woods today, you're sure of a big surprise. If you go down to the woods today, you better go in disguise. For every bear that ever there was, is gathered there for certain. Because . . .*"

"Don't sing that! That's an awful choice," Cody interrupted.

"Seemed appropriate to me."

He stifled a grin. "Fine."

They sang and they walked and maybe it worked, or maybe they got lucky. Either way, they puffed up a rugged series of humpback hills and burst out of the tunnel into the grey afternoon light.

"We made it," Samantha said.

"Awesome. We must be close."

"Which way?"

Ahead, a narrow track led through dry, waist-high grass. Bits of fur clung here and there. Beyond that, dark marshland, and further away, the upper lake. It gleamed silver, nestled between brush-covered knolls and high mountains.

"No sign of Treadwell, but I bet he's camped near the lake," Cody said. "He probably hides his tent."

"Let's leave our stuff here. I'm sick of carrying it."

They pushed their backpacks, tent, and sleeping bags into the brush and covered it all with leaves. Cody tagged the nearest tree with a strip from a plastic bag to mark the spot.

As they reached a knoll overlooking the lake, he spotted two green tents along the water.

"Those must be Treadwell's. Yay!" Cody said. "He's here."

"What a relief!" Samantha said. "But that's a crazy place to camp. Bears must walk right past the tents to get to the lake."

"I guess he isn't scared," Cody said. "Let's go."

They scrambled downward. Another few minutes and they'd be safe. They just had to reach Treadwell.

Something roared.

More roars. Grunts. Sharp, low woofs.

Cody's heart felt like it might burst out of his chest.

"Uh oh!" Samantha gasped.

Cody held his finger to his lips. "Shh."

The sound of running water gurgled and splashed nearby. Cody inched through the thick brush and came to a dead halt.

Treadwell's camp was in shouting distance, but between

them lay a fast-flowing creek. And it was crammed with bears. Very big bears. Dozens of them. All were focused on catching salmon. Some grizzlies hunted in pools on the creek's rocky banks and some were in the water.

"What now?" Samantha whispered.

A massive bear casually lifted a boulder and tossed it.

Splash!

Salmon scattered and the victorious bear grabbed a fish. Biting off the salmon's head, he tore into it, sliding the flesh off the bones like a kid downing a popsicle. Incredible.

From here, he could smell the musky bear's fishy breath. He and Samantha dropped low in the brush.

He couldn't believe it when Samantha pulled out her camera and grabbed a few snaps.

Then again, if they needed material for their project, this was it. They were seeing these amazing predators in a way few people did. They were in grizzly central.

Heart thumping with terror and excitement, Cody watched, fascinated, taking it all in. This was why they'd come—to see it for themselves.

They were too close, part of him knew that, but another part understood Treadwell one hundred percent. It was a rush, a dangerous rush.

A smaller grizzly roared and attacked another bear its size. They clashed and rolled to the ground, biting and wrestling. Were they fighting or playing? Competing for dominance? Muscles rippled and claws swiped. Water splashed and gravel scattered. Other bears growled and galloped back a few feet.

Samantha dug her fingers into his arm. "There's Tim," she whispered. "Over there."

Cody glanced at the far bank. Tim Treadwell, dressed in

sunglasses, black jeans, black bandana, and a black water-proof jacket, was crawling around on all fours.

What the heck was he doing?

"Weird," she said. "I think he's trying to look like a bear."

TEN

KATMAI NATIONAL PARK
UPPER KATMAI LAKE

Cody and Samantha watched from their hiding place.

Tim lumbered up on all fours to a cream-colored grizzly. Although it was a smaller bear, it was still enormous and powerful.

Tim leaned forward. Did he just kiss the grizzly's nose? Talk about taking a chance! That guy was out of control. Wait, was he singing? Cody strained to listen.

"Downy, Downy, you're such a beautiful bear," Tim sang in a high sing-song voice. *"Beautiful, beautiful Downy, you're my favorite bear. I'm so glad, Downy, that you are back at the maze."*

It was incredible. Downy seemed to accept Treadwell, for the bear plopped down right next to him!

This place, these beautiful, deadly-powerful animals, it was magical. And Treadwell was living right here with them. How? How did he get them to be his friends? To think Tim had survived thirteen summers!

Crunch.

Grunt.

The warning sounds came from a hundred yards up the bank. Cody and Samantha shrank lower.

From out of the alders, a massive dark-brown grizzly emerged from a tunnel and ambled down to the creek.

Tim spotted him, too. He waved. "Hey! Mr. Chocolate! Great to see you. Come on over. Your friend, Downy, is here."

Mr. Chocolate—the largest, most powerfully muscled bear Cody had ever imagined—studied Tim for a moment and then waded into the water. It began grabbing at the leaping salmon.

Mr. Chocolate was fierce but clumsy. While some bears caught fish after fish, Mr. Chocolate kept missing.

"Hey, Mr. Chocolate," Tim shouted. "You should do what Downy's doing. She's catching more than you." It was like he was talking to a pet dog!

Mr. Chocolate ignored him. Instead, the bear lowered his huge body into the water and sat. As the current rushed over him, he grabbed the salmon that were leaping right into his big, hairy chest. Now that was clever.

Cody stifled a chuckle. He loved these bears.

Without warning, two battle-scarred alpha bears galloped out of a bear tunnel.

Instantly, the Eden-like atmosphere changed.

"Get down," Cody whispered.

The massive grizzlies lumbered along the bank. The females and smaller bears moved out of the newcomers' way.

Tim obviously feared them, too, because his face changed. Still on all fours like a bear, he watched warily.

"Hi Machine! Hi Demon!" he called, his voice calm and low. "Everything okay with you, Demon? Do you come in peace, Demon?"

Machine? Demon?

As if to live up to his name, Demon rose on his haunches and charged at Tim.

Instead of running or playing dead, Tim held his ground, still on all fours in his bear costume. Was he crazy?

Demon lurched to a halt.

Whew!

The charge was fake.

Still, Demon and Tim faced off, staring at one another.

Suddenly, Tim leaped up, standing tall, arms stretched

overhead. He took a firm step forward. "Back, Demon," he warned. "Back now."

Clearly Tim was trying to show that he was more powerful. But he wasn't. Demon was monstrous—standing on his hind legs, he was tall enough to look through a second-floor window. With a head four times the size of a human skull, forty-two deadly teeth, paws the size of frying pans, and twenty razor-sharp claws.

An apex predator that could finish Tim with one swipe.

Did Demon know Tim was bluffing?

Demon opened his jaws and roared.

If only Cody had the rifle, he could fire into the air to create a distraction!

Face strained, Tim changed strategy. He sidestepped, slid down the bank into the creek, and swam, smooth but quick, to Mr. Chocolate.

Samantha whispered, "He's going to Mr. Chocolate for help!"

Cody held his breath. What a move! This was a real-life game of chess. And the strategy worked. With Mr. Chocolate at Tim's side, Demon lost interest in the battle.

The rest of the bears went back to fishing. It reminded him of the dog park. Some animals were peaceful, some were aggressive. Mr. Chocolate was the largest predator in the creek, yet he didn't need to prove himself. What a bear!

It seemed like a good moment to get Tim's attention.

Cody raised an arm and waved.

Tim didn't notice.

"We have to find a way to signal Tim," Cody whispered. "If we shout, Demon will hear, and who knows what'll happen."

Shivering, Samantha nodded.

They tried waving over and over, but they were too far, and he was too absorbed in his work. The excitement factor was wearing off, and the sweat from their walk had turned icy. More worrisome, though, the longer they sat here, the more danger they'd be in.

Samantha said, "There's no way. He doesn't see us, and Demon and Machine have control of the creek. We should go—wait for the bears to clear out. At least we know he's here."

"You're right."

They started back to where they'd left their camping stuff.

"How long do you think those bears will hang around the creek?" Samantha whispered, scanning for danger.

"I don't know. We better find a safe place to hang out for a few hours."

"How will we know it's a safe place?" she asked.

"Your guess is as good as mine."

"Those bears eat like they're starving," she murmured. "They didn't show that in the documentary."

"I guess they have to fatten up. Can you imagine sleeping for six or seven months without food? The clock is ticking. They're eating everything in sight before hibernation hits."

"Okay, I'm scared," she said.

"Who wouldn't be?"

This was nature in the raw.

Deep in the grass, something rustled.

ELEVEN

KATMAI NATIONAL PARK

Samantha froze. She wheeled around. "What was that?"

Cody tensed to listen. Was something stalking them? The cold air bit at his exposed cheeks. "I don't hear anything."

"Well, I did."

"You probably imagined it," he said.

"Oh sure, a mysterious noise. No point in worrying!" Samantha whispered.

"Probably a rabbit. Or a squirrel."

Grunt. Thud. Snort.

Bear.

Samantha practically climbed onto Cody's shoulders in terror.

It was too late to run; the predator was nearly there! Cody lunged sideways into the long grass, dragging his cousin with him.

"It'll smell us," she gasped.

Cody's fingers squished into something warm. An awful stench assaulted his nostrils. Bear poop.

"Quick," he whispered. "Rub this on your arms. It'll hide our smell."

Trembling and stinking, they waited.

A large grizzly rumbled out of a nearby tunnel. It neared their hiding spot and ground to a halt. The bear sniffed.

Cody closed his eyes and held his breath. His wet boots stank. Did the bear recognize the smell of human feet?

Time stopped.

The grizzly scratched the dirt, popped a wiggling worm into its mouth, and rumbled off.

When the coast was clear, they wiped themselves clean as best they could with leaves and grass and hurried on. At a creek, they washed their hands and kept going.

The tent and sleeping bags lay in the bushes where they'd left them. But it looked like a tornado had hit. All their stuff was shredded.

Cody stared. "Oh, for Pete's sake! That's the last of our food."

Samantha groaned. "It stinks! Everything's been peed on. Again! It had to be that fox. I can't believe it! What are we going to eat?"

Cody spotted the culprit—a red fox watching from the brush. Cody charged, and the thief streaked off, one of their socks between its teeth.

"The red fox strikes again," he muttered.

"Just grab what we can," Samantha said, peering skyward. "Uh oh, storm clouds."

With their smelly belongings rolled into two bundles,

they trekked until they reached an area protected by a massive boulder and an overhanging tree.

"This looks like our best bet." Cody dropped his pack.

"You think it's safe?"

His stomach growled. "I don't know, but I'm starving."

Samantha laughed. "I guess you should have had a bigger breakfast."

"Hey, it's way past lunch already. I'll backtrack to that creek and catch us a fish. Wait here."

"Not a chance," Samantha said. "I'm a better fisher."

It was safer to stick together anyway. Cody rummaged for the fishing lines.

"Bring the bear spray," Samantha said.

"Okay, and I'll bring the ax, too."

The creek gurgled and flashed. A rabbit hopped by. A squirrel chittered. Cody took it as a good sign—no bears on the hunt.

He formed a fishing rod from a branch and nylon line. Warily, he kept glancing over his shoulder and chanted. "I'm here, bear. Don't worry, bear, it's just me."

A salmon leaped out of the water and flew at him like an NFL player with the ball. Cody dropped his rod and made a grab. The slippery fish jumped clear.

Cody landed on his knees with a splash. Lucky Matt wasn't here to laugh at him being a klutz. Thinking of Matt, hopefully he was okay.

A bird swooped and made off with a fish. Great, even birds were better at fishing.

Fists on her hips, Samantha assessed the creek. After a moment, she waded into the water, hands cupped, and herded a salmon beneath an overhanging bank. Triumphant, she grasped the fish to her chest and grinned.

"Yes!" Cody cried, running to help. "Don't lose it, well done!"

They scrambled ashore.

"I'll clean it," he offered.

"Do it quick before a bear smells it and comes running."

Cody scaled and cleaned the salmon like Gramps had taught him. He was finishing in record time when the alders shook, and a massive form lumbered into view. A grizzly. Hunched. Ears back.

Cody's blood ran cold.

The grizzly closed in, picking up speed.

It was happening fast, but Cody's terror turned everything into slow motion. Like a close-up in a horror movie, the immense furry face with long scars came into focus.

"Back!" Cody yelled, stomping and sending pebbles scattering. "Get back! Don't even think about it!"

The grizzly roared. Slobber dripped from its jaws.

Samantha moved to his side. "Aaaargh!" she yelled. "Get away! Go!"

Cody pitched the salmon like a fastball, straight at the

bear's head.

Smack!

It hit the grizzly right in the snout.

As one, Cody and Samantha yelled and waved and stomped. "Get away! Back! Back! Now!"

The grizzly lunged.

"The spray!" Samantha screamed.

Thankful he'd stuck it in his jacket pocket, Cody grabbed the can. He blasted the bear with an orange cloud. The grizzly reeled, spinning sideways. It coughed, ran, and rolled its head in the grass.

Enraged, the grizzly pulled itself up. The animal was going to charge again.

"Blast it!" Samantha screamed. "Blast it!"

Cody sprayed again.

The bear roared with rage and pain. Then it pivoted and disappeared into the dark.

Cody's teeth chattered. "Holy moly, that thing was massive. Even on all fours, it was taller than my head. One swipe of those paws could knock down a moose."

Still gripping the spray, he squinted into the dark trees.

Samantha looked ruefully at the salmon lying in the mud. "Guess that's the end of the salmon."

"No way." Cody brushed off the mud and rinsed it in the creek. "Let's go before he returns."

Samantha grabbed his elbow. "Uh, Cody?"

To his horror, another monster male rose out of the brush. The cousins backpedaled. This bear locked eyes with him. Cody dropped his glance and kept retreating. To his relief, maybe this was one of those bears Gramps mentioned, the kind that didn't like meeting humans, for it crashed away into the brush.

Samantha shivered. "I'm not going anywhere with that fish." Her voice had that stubborn tone that he knew so well.

But she was talking about his lunch and probably even his dinner.

"The fish won't be around long because I'm going to eat it," he said. "We can't hike miles and escape from bears if we don't eat."

Samantha glared. "Then hand over the spray. I'm keeping it in *my* jacket pocket."

"Suit yourself."

They hurried back to the tent. Samantha stood guard while he made a fire. The flames blazed bright and hot, sizzling as the first raindrops began to fall.

"That should help. Bears don't like fire." Cody speared pieces of salmon and blackened them. He handed some to Samantha, and they both tore into it like starving animals.

Samantha said, "Sort of raw."

"Sashimi," Cody said. "It would cost a fortune in Malibu."

She licked her lips. "I must be hungry because it's the best thing I ever tasted." She jumped as a gust of wind rattled the grass. "Whoa, that spooked me. How can Tim live here?"

That's when the downpour hit. They dove into the tent and zipped up the door.

"What if he decides to fly out early? Because of the storm? We need to get to him," Cody said.

"The minute the rain lets up, we'll head to his camp."

In the dim light, they eyed one another, suddenly serious. Then he said what they both were clearly thinking.

"If we get stuck here, we're doomed."

TWELVE

K<small>ATMAI</small> N<small>ATIONAL</small> P<small>ARK</small>

As night fell, the storm only grew more violent. Temperatures dropped fast. At least the tent felt snug and dry. No one was going anywhere in this weather.

Cody had just curled up in his sleeping bag when Samantha shook his shoulder.

"I need to pee."

"Do it far from the tent," Cody muttered.

Samantha shook his shoulder again. "You have to come with me."

"No way I'm going out there again."

"Please," Samantha begged.

Cody groaned. "Just go by yourself and do it quickly."

"No!" Samantha wailed.

"You have to. And bury it. Or the bears will smell it. Cover it with dirt."

"Don't be mean. I'm not going out there alone."

Cody groaned. Flashlight in hand, he crawled out of the tent. Samantha followed. The wind whipped rain into his face.

"Hurry," Cody said. "I'll keep watch."

As she peed, Cody turned his back and shone the flashlight into the flurry of raindrops.

Two eyes shone back.

"Bear!" Samantha gasped and scrambled up.

"Stay still," Cody murmured. "Whatever you do, don't run."

The bear, his fur drenched, melted away into the trees.

Inside the tent, Cody lay shivering. He could hear Samantha's teeth chattering. Yikes, this place was cold. He wrapped his arms around his chest and listened to the downpour. Cody had never been so cold. His feet were frozen. He opened his sturdy Kevlar backpack and stuffed his feet—still in the sleeping bag—into it for extra protection. The backpack helped.

Outside, a twig snapped.

Like a jack-in-the-box, he sat up. Numbskull! They should have pitched the tent further from the maze.

"What was that?" Samantha whispered.

"Something's out there."

Something out of his worst nightmares. The tent shuddered and a monster head, haloed by a flash of lightning, burst through the flap. Giant snout. Shiny nose. Bulging jaws. Long teeth. Steaming breath, reeking of fish.

"Get away!" Cody shouted. "Get lost! Get out!"

Time stood still.

Lightning flashed again. The grizzly stared, eyes cold. Focused. Saliva drooling from its powerful jaws.

"Get out!" Samantha shrieked in the sudden darkness. "Get *out!*"

Her screams worked. When lightning flashed again, the monster head had disappeared.

"Whoa," Samantha breathed.

"Stay still," Cody hissed.

"I think it's gone," Samantha whispered. "I almost had a heart attack."

"Me too." Cody let out a nervous snort. "That was crazy. Too bad you didn't get a photo."

Samantha switched on her flashlight. "Did we scare it away?"

"Must have."

Without warning, a paw the size of a giant's baseball mitt ripped through the nylon. Dagger-like, three-inch-long claws swiped just inches from his nose.

"The spray," Cody yelled. Frantic, he rolled around,

trying to find it while Samantha fumbled in her bag.

The grizzly clawed at the tent again, tearing another hole in the nylon.

"Get!" he screamed. "Get away, bear!"

One side of the tent caved inward. The grizzly's muzzle was outlined by the fabric. It lunged and bit downward. The massive jaws, weirdly hidden by the collapsing tent wall, closed around Cody's Kevlar backpack—with Cody's feet trapped inside!

"My legs!" Cody shouted.

The jaws squeezed tighter and tighter until his legs went numb.

"Get away!" he screamed, punching the fabric-clad head. "Get away!"

The grizzly squeezed harder. Pushing, pushing down. Did it think it had him by the neck? Did it think it was killing him? He could hear the grizzly's heavy, huffing breath.

"Get out of the sleeping bag!" Samantha shrieked.

"I can't! The zipper's stuck." Frantic now, Cody pulled at the zipper.

"Hit it!" she shouted, whacking it with the flashlight.

Wildly, Cody felt around for a weapon. His fingers closed over the iron pot. He beat at the bear's head. Hard. Over and over until he was sure the bear's skull would break.

The bear pulled back.

Rain spattered through the tent's gaping holes. Cody waited, every muscle tensed for survival.

The only sounds came from the cold downpour and the wailing wind.

The bear had gone.

"Are you okay?" Samantha whispered.

The flashlight illuminated the Kevlar bag. He wiggled his toes. "A bit numb, that's all. No wonder they use Kevlar for attack dog training. It worked for grizzly teeth, too. It saved my legs."

Samantha's face shone pale. "I wish we had full body armor right now. Do you think it's going to come back?"

"I don't know." Cody shone the light on the rips. The moisture along the edges was already turning to ice. The wind howled like a banshee, drenching everything inside. "We better fix this tent, though. Otherwise, we'll freeze to death."

He dug out some fishing line and a hook. Together, the cousins patched the tears as best they could. Then they huddled into the one corner that was still dry.

"Let's take turns keeping watch," he said.

"Good idea."

"I'll take the first shift."

Samantha nodded. But even after thirty minutes, he could tell from her breathing that she wasn't asleep.

So far, they'd been lucky. Incredibly lucky. With a sinking feeling, Cody knew their luck couldn't hold much longer.

And what about Matt? Was he all right?

They had to survive the night. They had to make their way to Treadwell's camp. They had to get a hold of his sat phone and call that pilot.

They'd been warned it was too dangerous to come. Multiple times by multiple people. Cody had ignored them and every instinct because of money—because Matt had bought those tickets.

If he could go back in time, knowing what he knew now, he'd gladly throw them away to be safely at Gramps.

THIRTEEN

KATMAI NATIONAL PARK

A feral shriek broke the silence. A gut-wrenching shriek.

Cody woke with a start, cursing himself for drifting off, and blinked in the weak pre-dawn light.

Samantha popped up. "What was that?"

"I don't know. A rabbit? A fox?"

"Poor creature," Samantha said. "I wonder what's happening to it."

The shrieks abruptly died out. Somewhere, an owl hooted, and other noises joined in. A pre-dawn chorus of tweets, chirps, whistles, and calls.

"Last night was a nightmare," Samantha said. "I thought we were finished."

Cody grimaced. "Me too."

"At least there's some good news."

"Really?" Cody said, surprised.

She triumphantly produced a chocolate peanut butter

protein bar. "Look what I found. It was at the bottom of my bag. Your fave."

"You're kidding!"

She unwrapped the bar and handed him half.

"Yum!" Cody ate his share, savoring every bite. He was still hungry, but at least his stomach wasn't gnawing. "We better get moving."

The cousins rolled up their sleeping bags and crawled out of their ripped tent.

Cody inhaled sharply. "Check out those bear prints! They're huge. And not just one bear. Lots of bears. All prowling round our tent."

"I can't believe we survived." Samantha shuddered.

Cody picked up the ax, and Samantha pocketed the bear spray.

"Let's head back to Treadwell's camp. Hopefully, this time we can reach him."

"Fingers crossed," Samantha said.

Cody grinned. "Maybe he has some breakfast to share."

"Dream on," Samantha said.

"Eggs, pancakes, and double bacon work for me." Cody led the way, ax ready for action.

After an hour, Cody stopped. "We're lost."

"We should have found the river ages ago," she said.

They kept walking. The ground grew steeper, and after another hour, they'd climbed to a high point above the river. Cody pulled out his binoculars and searched the terrain below.

"I see it, there's Treadwell's camp."

It had to be at least a mile away. The river looked totally different this morning—no bears fishing, no bears fighting, just rushing water beneath a red-dawn sky.

Tim's two tents were still in the same spot.

"They're probably still asleep," he whispered.

"They wouldn't hear us even if we shouted," Samantha said, taking a turn with the binoculars before handing them back.

"Whoa. What the heck?" Cody said, watching Treadwell's camp for signs of movement. "There's a grizzly down there, right behind his tent."

"Let me see! Uh oh. Something's wrong with it," Samantha said.

An emaciated grizzly lay by the larger tent. It shook its head as if to ward off a fly and rose to its haunches with difficulty. Moving slowly, it inched toward the water, dragging one of its back legs.

"It's injured," Cody said.

The grizzly made it a few more feet, then dropped to its belly and lay there.

"And I see more bears," Cody added, "In the grass. I just noticed them. A mother grizzly with two cubs. I bet Treadwell's feeding them and that injured one."

"Pretty risky, but I guess he knows what he's doing."

"I guess so. Let's climb down this way and see if we can head in his direction."

"Okay. Maybe we'll find some berries, too," Samantha said. "I'm starving."

Ax in hand, Cody hacked a trail through the brush and grass. Things felt better this morning, easier. He was sure they could get Treadwell's attention today now that the river was mostly empty.

Once they used his sat phone to contact their pilot, the plane would be here in no time. They'd be on that flight and back to civilization early afternoon. And tonight, they'd be at Gramps' cabin. All of this would be an incredible survival story to tell their friends.

He walked with a spring in his step and cheered when they found a small patch of blueberries.

The ground started to rise again.

He slowed.

It shouldn't be going up.

Samantha said, "We should be there by now."

All around them, trees, boulders, and brush offered no clue which way to go.

"Let's keep walking."

It was hard to judge how much time had passed. Every path they chose took them closer to the jagged, snow-topped mountains. Big, dark clouds rolled down the sheer cliffs, surrounding them in a thick gray blur.

They broke free from the shelter of the alders and the wind blew hard, almost gale force.

"Snow!" Cody pulled up his jacket hood as snowflakes whirled.

"I'm freezing." Samantha shuddered.

The trail led gradually uphill. The mountains loomed above them.

"Maybe if we get higher, we can figure out where we are," Cody said.

Climbing steadily, soon they were huffing. They needed a break. They'd been hiking for hours in the cold on half a protein bar and a handful of berries. And if they didn't warm up soon, they'd be in trouble.

"See that dark spot in the cliff? That's a cave." Samantha said.

Cody squinted. "Yeah. That could work. As long as no bears live there. Hold on, I'll climb up and check."

As he scrambled up the rocks, the half-frozen mud under his feet gave way.

Samantha grabbed him.

And they both went sliding.

FOURTEEN

K<small>ATMAI</small> N<small>ATIONAL</small> P<small>ARK</small>

Cody slid fast, hurtling between two sheer rock walls. Jagged rocks reared up in front of him. Grunting, he threw his body right and left, moving like a snowboarder to try and avoid them.

A huge boulder loomed. He wrapped his arms around his head, and his body spun. Suddenly he was somersaulting in a terrifying blur, like some mad stuntman.

Bang!

Thump!

His shoulder smashed into a rock, his butt into another. Bone-jarring hits that left him gasping. He lay, winded, in a mess of mud, rocks, and rubble.

Shrieking, Samantha landed on top of him.

They untangled their limbs and lay there puffing.

"Are you okay?" Cody said.

"Sort of. Ow! My ribs kill." Samantha grimaced. "Uh oh. Look how far we fell."

"I know. We're going to have to hike back up. This gorge is just some kind of rock crevice."

"Seriously?"

Cody nodded. At least Samantha wasn't blaming him.

As they stared upward, fresh gusts of snow, hurled by the wind, blinded them.

"We're stuck in the snow like the Donner Party," Samantha said.

"You mean the dudes who ate each other?"

Samantha tried to laugh through her chattering teeth. She wiped the mud from her face, which only made it worse. "I'm freezing. We better wait until the snow stops. The first rule of survival is shelter."

"Right." The gorge ended abruptly in a cliff about sixty feet wide. Cody scanned the cliff face. Yes! A dark slot. "A cave!"

Samantha's brows arched in worry. "That one looks big enough for a grizzly den."

"I'll check it out," Cody said. "Carefully, this time." He rubbed his throbbing shoulder and stood. "Wait here."

"No way," Samantha said.

"I'll be right back."

Samantha scoffed. "Famous last words heard in every horror movie. I'm coming with you."

After a difficult scramble, they reached the cave mouth and peered inside. He paused, trying to adjust his eyes to the dark. The blackness was eerily quiet. All he could hear was his heart beating in his ears.

He took a step inside, and something hard cracked under his boot. Keeling, he picked up a half-gnawed bone.

There were more bones. The whole entrance was littered with them.

A violent gust of wind nearly sent him toppling. Gusts hurled snow and grit into his eyes.

Bones or not, he'd heard no animal sounds. Whatever lived here wasn't home. Hopefully, they wouldn't come home for a while, at least not until the storm died down.

He almost had to shout to be heard over the gale. "Let's go inside."

"I'm right behind you," Samantha shouted back. "Yell if you see a bear!"

"You got it."

Heart in his throat, he led the way back into the cave.

Faraway, something howled, long and clear. Followed by a chorus of deep barks and short high-pitched howls. The hair on the back of Cody's neck stood on end. "Wolves."

"Is this their den?" Samantha's voice shook.

"I don't know," Cody said.

Samantha grabbed his arm. "Something's coming in!"

Frantic, Cody felt for the ax. Wasn't there.

A big head poked into the cave. It wasn't a grizzly; he could see from the shape. A horse? Wow, a horse would be great. For one glorious moment, he pictured himself riding out of the wilderness like Wyatt Earp.

No. The head was bigger than a horse.

Through the gale, he made out the shape of antlers. "A moose!" He grinned. "They're vegetarian. Won't eat us. Hey, big guy!"

The moose couldn't quite fit inside. It sniffed around, let out a disgusted snort, pulled its head back, and left.

"He didn't like your smell," Samantha said.

"Ha!" Cody sank down onto his backpack. "The ground

seems clean enough and there's piles of dry grass. Burrow into it. It'll keep us warmer."

"A grizzly probably brought that grass in here." Samantha said. "These are some grizzly family's beds."

Cody pictured a bear family in here with their cubs. That must be quite a sight. Adult bears were terrifying, but the cubs must look pretty cute all curled into balls.

After a moment, he said, "Well, the bears aren't home now and I don't see that we have any other choice. I'm lying in one."

Samantha took a deep breath. "Okay. You have a good point there. I kind of feel like Goldilocks, though. Too bad there's no porridge in this place."

"Ha ha, that would be good." Cody burrowed into the grass. "Grizzlies sure know how to hibernate. This is pretty comfy. Did you know that when they're hibernating, not only do they not eat, they don't pee or poo either."

"Really? Wow!" Samantha said. "Too bad I'm not a grizzly."

Samantha burrowed into her own pile. "This grass is dry enough to light a fire."

"You're right. That's a really good idea. Come on, help me make a fire."

They gathered a small pile near the entrance, and Cody flicked the lighter. A flame rose. Shivering, they huddled close to the crackling warmth. In the yellow light, Cody spotted branches further back that must have blown in here with the wind. He gathered an armful and fed a few to the flames.

"That's better," Samantha said. "Safer too. Though I wish we were at Gramp's cabin."

"Yeah," Cody agreed. "Cozy and chilling on the sofa. When we planned this, I sure didn't think we would end up this way."

"Don't say *end*." Samantha groaned. "I'm too tired to be scared anymore."

"Okay," Cody agreed. "Let's think about the great story we'll have for our school projects. Or we can plan our project for next year. I vote we do one at Disney World."

Samantha laughed. "Yeah. We'll watch the Bear Jamboree. Much safer!"

"And better food."

They grinned at one another.

"What would you eat right now if you could have anything?" Samantha asked.

"A burger—a huge, juicy burger on a soft bun. With melted cheese. Mustard. Ketchup. Pickles. A massive pile of crispy fries. And lemonade. Mom's homemade lemonade—sweet, with a dash of sour."

"Stop!" Samantha laughed. "I can't take it."

Too hungry to think, Cody climbed back into his straw bed, and Samantha did the same.

FIFTEEN

KATMAI NATIONAL PARK

Pink light was streaming into the cave when Cody blinked awake. He couldn't feel his feet. He thought of the Everest explorers who'd lost their limbs to hyperthermia. Quickly, he flexed his hands and toes.

"You woke me!" Samantha muttered. "What's all that noise?"

Cody blew on his throbbing fingers. "I'm freezing."

"What time is it?"

"Must be morning, we slept all night."

The air smelled smoky, and their fire was a mess of black coals. The stench must have kept predators away. At least they'd stayed alive two whole nights alone. That had to be worth something.

"Do you think Matt's okay?" Samantha asked.

"I hope so. Let's go. We can't afford to get lost again.

We'll find Treadwell this time," he said, trying to sound sure.

Samantha didn't reply.

Again, he remembered they'd told no one they were up here. They'd ignored one of the most important rules of survival: Make sure people know where you are.

Cody felt woozy from hunger and thirst but tried to ignore it. Samantha didn't mention food; she had to be starving, too.

They stumbled out of the cave and landed in a snow-bank. Fluffy snowdrifts covered everything.

A horrible thought ripped through his brain. "The storm's over. What if Tim calls his pilot to pick him up today? Instead of waiting until the end of the week? More bad weather might be coming."

Samantha blanched. "Let's go. Fast."

Cody studied the cliff. "No way we can climb back up that way now. There's a frozen overhang. We'll start an avalanche. We'll have to try that other section and hope it leads out."

"It's almost as steep as the cliff," Samantha protested.

"Only way to go," Cody said. "Come on."

Samantha groaned and tightened her backpack.

With his boots sinking into knee-high snowdrifts, Cody grabbed one snowy branch after another and hauled himself along. Climbing. Crawling. Sliding. Behind him, he heard Samantha puffing.

"Cody, look at those tracks! Big hoofs—must be from the moose."

"Yeah, and did you see those over there? Paw prints in single file. Wolves."

"Can you believe they walk in single file like that? I'm glad we weren't stuck outside last night." She licked her dry lips. "I'm so thirsty. Do you think it's okay to eat snow?"

"I guess. As long as it's not yellow."

"Funny, aren't you!" She nibbled at a handful of snow. "It's making me even colder."

Nervous tension filled him. He pictured the floatplane arriving early and carrying Tim and Amie back to Kodiak. He pictured it flying overhead, off to the safety of civilization. To dry hotel rooms and noisy restaurants and hot showers.

He pictured himself, Samantha, and Matt stuck alone, trying to find food and escape bears for seven long months.

They'd never make it.

"We have to get out of these snowdrifts," he called, heading over to a flat section of snow.

Too late, he realized his mistake. What he'd thought was a shallow ditch was a snow hole. The snow gave way beneath him, and he was falling all over again. Except that this time, it was worse. He was falling through thin air, plunging into darkness. Down he went.

Oof!

He landed hard against a snowy slope. Digging in, his heels hit something solid, and he jolted to a stop. The impact forced the air from his lungs. Yikes! The snow hole was deep, and he was only halfway down. All that supported him was a wedge of hard ice. If the wedge collapsed, he'd fall further and never get out.

Looking up, he saw daylight and Samantha's worry-scrunched face peering down.

"Are you hurt?" she shouted.

"Don't stand there!" Cody yelled. "The whole thing could collapse."

"Okay. I'll lie flat. Can you climb out?"

"I don't know. I'm afraid to move."

"I can't reach you. I wish we had a rope."

He felt weak, not his usual self. Worse, time was ticking—what if Tim's plane came?

For a minute, there was silence. Cody took a deep breath and winced as the frigid air hit his dry throat.

"Samantha, you should keep going," he called. "You can come back for me."

Maybe he'd never get out. The snow hole was an icy tomb.

"Try and climb out!" she called. "You can do it. Baby steps. One foot after another. Start! Now!"

"It's too steep and slippery." Still, he began to climb, cramming his cold, aching hands and feet into the icy walls. Every time he moved a few feet, he'd slip several inches. He was making progress but barely.

If he fell, he'd be history. His heart jack-hammered.

"Here!" Samantha pulled the strap off her backpack and extended it to its full length. With both arms outstretched, she dangled it down. "Can you reach this? I'll pull you out."

"It's too far."

"Keep climbing."

Cody struggled upward. Finally, the strap was within reach. He grabbed it with fingers that were weak from exertion. "Don't fall in, too."

"I won't." Samantha's voice trembled.

"I'm too heavy for you," Cody whispered through dry lips.

"Hang on to the strap with one hand and keep climbing."

Inch by inch, Cody climbed.

With a final grunt, Samantha took one hand off the strap and grabbed his arm. As she leaned back, tugging, Cody braced his knees and pushed. He threw one hand over the ledge, then the other. He was out.

They lay in the snow, gasping.

Samantha said, "Hey, no more falling, okay?"

"Deal. I thought I was gone. Thanks, cousin. I owe you." He rubbed his twisted knee. "Let's move. Faster the better."

Limping, he headed off. Coming out of the trees, he got a bird's-eye-view of the lake. It rippled below, like a shining plate of steel.

The day was way past noon when they reached the top of the gorge.

They paused to take in the sight. The air felt so much warmer down here, and it felt good to be on level ground. Even better, Cody was sure he recognized this place.

"I think we're close to Treadwell's camp. That's where we stored our camping gear the other day when we first came looking for him."

"You're right!"

"And I haven't heard any airplanes. We would have heard if one had come for him. So he has to still be here."

They both blew out relieved sighs.

Samantha pulled the brambles aside, searching for berries. "No wonder the bears are fighting for salmon. There's nothing else to eat."

"I'm so thirsty. I wonder how Matt is doing."

"He had those cans of beer," Samantha said. "He's probably drunk."

"I read a survival quiz," Cody puffed. "If your plane crashes and you only have beer, do you drink it?"

"I guess." Samantha started walking.

"The correct answer is no. Alcohol dehydrates you."

"Huh! What other questions were there?"

Cody cleared the painful dryness from his throat and croaked. "Your plane runs out of fuel over the desert. As the plane descends, you spot a hut. Do you hike to the hut?"

Samantha thought for a minute. "Yes."

"Nope," Cody replied. "The answer is to stay with the plane or vehicle so rescuers can find you."

"Well, going by that advice, we should have stayed at the lower lake where our pilot left us."

"Maybe," Cody admitted. "Except no one knows we need rescuing."

Faces grim, they kept moving.

A scream shattered the silence. "Get! Get away! You heard me—get away!"

Cody spun round. "What was that?

Samantha grabbed his arm. "It sounded like Matt."

"Did it?"

Wide-eyed, they stared at each other.

"Help! Help me!" the voice screamed. "I'm being killed out here. Help me!"

SIXTEEN

K<small>ATMAI</small> N<small>ATIONAL</small> P<small>ARK</small>

"W-what's happening?" Samantha stuttered. "Where is he?"

"I don't know. He's being attacked! Sounds like he's somewhere in the maze."

"Oh no, Cody! He must have come looking for us."

The screaming changed from words to incoherent screeches. Wild yells, mixed with the wail of the wind.

Samantha's face screwed up with fear. "Sounds like a bear has him."

Shrill, agonized shrieks made Cody's stomach lurch. He had to help his cousin, but he'd lost the ax and Matt had the rifle.

Why didn't Matt shoot?

With Samantha on his heels, Cody thrust through the thick grass stalks. They followed the high, horrible, keening sound, running toward trouble, desperate to try and help.

As suddenly as it started, the screaming stopped.

The silence was deafening. With awful pictures racing through his mind, Cody flashed a look at Samantha.

Her face was ashen. "Oh Cody, what's happened?"

"We have to find him." As he ran, Cody thought of Matt.

His cousin hadn't always been a jerk. When they were little, they'd been friends. Their moms took them to the local park on weekends. Matt had been fun to play with.

What had made Matt change? Why had he become a bully?

He flashed back to a day in the park when Uncle John reluctantly came along for the ride. Matt fell off a swing. He hit the ground hard and started crying. His dad shouted that he was acting like a baby and he'd give him something to cry about.

Uncle John was a heavy drinker. He got mean when he drank, and that day he'd been putting away can after can of beer.

Now, as Cody ran, the thwack-thwack of his boots reminded him of Uncle John's angry smacks. Poor Matt. Even as a little kid, Cody had been shocked. His own dad would never have done that. His dad would have picked him up and made him feel safe. A year later, Uncle John left. Aunt Lucy said she didn't care, but Cody knew that Matt did. That must have been awful.

Cody kept running. They flew out of the maze and came to a halt. It felt like weeks since the pilot had dropped them off in this lost place.

In the distance, he spotted Matt's blue tent down the beach. So alone and small in the wild.

He forced his injured leg to move faster—he had to help his cousin, even though his brain warned that it didn't make sense. Matt wouldn't be in the tent. They'd heard him way back, somewhere in the maze.

"Wait!" Samantha puffed. "Check for bears."

"I don't see any."

Together, they ran, scanning left and right.

As Cody neared the tent, he heard muffled sobs. Hysterical but soft, as if someone was sobbing but trying not to be heard.

Matt, he was alive! How?

Terrified of what he'd see, expecting to witness a bloody mess, Cody lifted the tent flap.

Inside, Matt cowered, his sleeping bag pressed to his face.

No sign of blood; the bear must have gotten his legs or something. As Matt sobbed, his body shook. Cody scrambled inside and touched his cousin's shoulder.

Matt spun around, rifle in hand.

"Whoa!" Cody leaped back. "Put that rifle down. It's me. Are you hurt?"

"No." Matt still waved the rifle.

"Put that away!" Cody said, thrusting the barrel to the side.

Samantha looked Matt over in confusion. "We heard you screaming. It sounded like—"

"I wasn't screaming," Matt said. "I heard *you* screaming. I thought a grizzly was attacking you."

Samantha shoved her fingers through her hair, her eyes baffled. "We thought it was you."

"Well, it wasn't," Matt said. "But it could have been." He wiped his swollen eyes. "I went through that stupid maze looking for you. When I got to the other side, I thought a grizzly had you both. I thought it would come for me next. So, I ran all the way back here. Worst experience I ever had."

"Tell us what you heard," Cody said.

"Like I told you, I got to the other side of the maze, near this river—"

"I meant, what did you hear?"

"First, a guy shouted for help," Matt said. "Then he screamed, *Hit it! Hit it with the pan!* Then he shouted, *Run! Run! Save yourself.*"

A nauseous feeling rose in Cody's throat. It seemed impossible. "That must have been Tim and Amie. A grizzly must have attacked them."

"But Tim has lived with bears for years," Samantha said. "He knows how to handle them."

"Some of those big bears didn't seem like his friends," Cody said. "That Demon looked downright deadly."

Matt shook his head. "It wasn't Treadwell. I saw the guy just before. He was down at the lake."

"You saw him?" Cody said.

"Sure did."

Samantha said, "Maybe it was one of those poachers. You saw Tim? Did you tell him we need help?"

"Nope. Couldn't get near him. Crazy dude was standing in the middle of some huge bears. Flipping out, saying how he much loved them and how he hated the hunters and poachers."

"Well, someone was attacked. You have the rifle, Matt. Why didn't you at least fire it?" Cody said. "That might have scared it off."

Matt's face turned red. "Yeah. I thought of firing the rifle. But I didn't want the grizzlies to know I was here. Anyway, it ended fast. After about five minutes, the screams stopped."

Five minutes? Cody stared at him. Five minutes was tons of time to fire a rifle.

Matt said, "Don't look at me like that. I want to get out of here alive. If you're smart, you do, too."

SEVENTEEN

KATMAI NATIONAL PARK

"Do you have any food left?" Cody asked.

"Ate it all. I was hoping you had some."

"We left it all with you, remember?" Cody said. "Listen, I'm going to get going. Give me the rifle."

"What for?" Matt said. "Where are you going?"

Seriously?

"To Treadwell's camp. So I can call for a plane."

Matt said, "Good luck with that, some maniac grizzly is on the prowl. You want to get killed?"

"No, but I don't want to get stuck here by the winter."

Samantha swallowed hard. "Matt's right. There's a dangerous animal out there."

"I have to go," Cody said, trying to sound confident. It didn't work. "Don't worry. I'll stay out of sight. I won't be long. You have the bear spray."

"I'm coming with you," Samantha said. "We've stuck together this long. I'm not letting you go alone."

Cody shook his head. "No, really. You don't have to."

"Wanna bet?" Samantha scrambled out of the tent after him. "Two heroes are safer than one."

Wide-eyed, she stared at the sky. Dark against the gray clouds, vultures circled. "Oh Cody, look—vultures! That's scary. Vultures circle when something is dead."

"Or badly injured," Cody said. "Stay here, please? Your parents will kill me if something happens to you."

"Don't play all macho. I'm going with you, dork."

Cody rolled his eyes.

From inside the tent, Matt shouted, "Hurry up and get back here. I don't want that bear to come after me."

Samantha said, "You've got the bear spray. Just remember to use it."

They headed off as fresh rain began to fall.

Soon it fell in a steady stream, pouring down their necks as they crept through the maze. What a miserable place!

Cody wiped rain out of his eyes and came to a grinding halt. Fifty yards away, a massive grizzly crouched over a pile of clothes. A leather jacket, jeans. Head down, it chewed.

Paralyzed with fear, Cody backed away.

Slowly. One foot behind the other. Quiet as a mouse . . .

His right heel caught on a rock.

With a gulp, he flung out his arms. Staggered.

Stones skittered, rattling across the wet ground.

The grizzly looked up. Eyes gleaming and far apart, locked on Cody. The massive animal reared up, each forearm bigger than Cody's whole body.

The bear roared.

Was the grizzly defending its meal? Were those more than just clothes?

Don't look into its eyes. Don't challenge it. It isn't after you. It thinks you're after its prey.

Cody inched away. Right into Samantha.

"Cody?" she whispered in a trembling voice.

He spoke softly. "Keep backing up."

Together, they crept out of view.

Once they were deep in the brush, he whispered. "I think that grizzly might have killed someone."

"Now what?" She sounded close to tears. "Oh Cody, we're dead, aren't we?"

"No." He had to focus, he couldn't give in to fear. "Come on. We'll take a different tunnel. Quietly."

Heart thumping, Cody led them on a circuitous route toward Treadwell's campsite. At the knoll, the silence was eerie—as if even animals were avoiding the place. He stared, appalled.

"What happened over there?" Samantha gasped.

Both tents were mashed flat.

There was no sign of Tim or Amie.

"I don't know." Stomach churning, Cody found a shallow spot in the river. They waded across, the water rising over their ankles.

A dark wet patch shone in front of the squashed big

tent. It was either mud or something awful, something he didn't want to think about.

Holding his breath, he lifted the tent canvas. Inside lay scattered clothes, water bottles, video camera equipment, sleeping bags, and a teddy bear. The fearless Tim Treadwell slept with a teddy bear.

Cody blinked hard as tears filled his eyes. "They're not here."

Samantha's face was ashen. "They might have gotten away."

"I don't think so," Cody said. "That leather jacket I saw on the trail, it looked like his. But Amie could still be alive. She may be hurt and hiding."

"If I was her, I'd stay hidden," Samantha said.

"I wonder if he called for help?" Cody said.

"Oh no," she said.

"What?"

"I hope he called for help before this happened," she said, striding toward a smashed object on the ground. She picked it up and showed him the broken remains.

"Is that his satellite phone? Oh no."

In the grass, a shadow moved. Something was watching.

Cody's skin prickled.

Then, the injured bear, the one he'd seen through the binoculars, limped into the campsite. It probably wanted Tim's help. This might be when Tim usually fed the bear.

Despite everything, Cody felt for the poor creature. It would have to fend for itself now.

"Let's go. We better regroup with Matt and come up with a new plan."

EIGHTEEN

Katmai National Park

"What took you so long?" Matt asked when they arrived back at the beach.

"I think Treadwell is dead."

Matt stared at Cody. "You can't be serious."

"I think Treadwell is dead and there's no way to call anyone."

"Now what?" Matt wailed.

"You're asking me? You're the one who bought the tickets. You're the one who dropped the sat phone—"

Samantha cut in. "Quit it, you guys. I'd like to get out of here alive, if possible? So someone better come up with a plan."

Cody and Matt glared at one another. After a long moment, Cody backed down.

"You're right," he said, his shoulders dropping. "All I

know is that his ride back is flying here soon. We're just going to have to wait it out."

"How long's that gonna take?" Matt said.

Cody squinted at the sky. Clouds towered like mountains, moving ominously overhead. "I don't know."

As he spoke, he focused on a black dot moving along the horizon. Had to be a bird. The dot headed steadily toward them. A low droning noise blended with the wind.

Samantha grabbed Cody's arm. "That's a plane!"

Cody whooped. "We're saved!"

Even Matt cheered.

Then, an awful thought struck. "It'll go to the upper lake," Cody said. "Treadwell's pilot doesn't know we're here."

Samantha's eyes went wide in panic. "Run," she gasped. "Let's go."

All three started toward the maze when Cody stopped.

"No," he said, sick with a fresh realization that they were about to make a deadly mistake. "We don't know what the pickup spot is. What if Treadwell told the pilot to meet him here?"

"Oh, wow, you're right," Samantha said. "Matt, stay here."

"No way."

Cody said, "There's no time! Look, Samantha, you stay here with Matt and I'll run. Okay?"

"Forget it, I'll go," she said.

"Just give me the rifle and make sure Matt doesn't do anything stupid. You know he won't stay here alone."

"I'm keeping the gun!" Matt shouted.

Cody ignored him and grabbed the rifle. He left a stunned and furious Samantha holding her bear mace and staring after him as he darted alone into the maze.

One last run. One last time.

This was the sprint that counted.

He only hoped he could make it.

NINETEEN

K<small>ATMAI</small> N<small>ATIONAL</small> P<small>ARK</small>

Cody knew his way by now. He took the long route, knowing it was the safest, even if his knee ached.

Overhead, the plane roared ever closer, circling for a landing.

Cody picked up speed, his too-large boot caught on a rock, and he went flying. He'd always been cursed with clumsiness. He landed hard on his injured leg just as a huge grizzly ambled down the tunnel.

Cody felt for the rifle and realized it had gone flying.

The bear paused and stared, tilting its head to one side as if trying to recognize him. It reminded Cody of a friendly dog.

Wait. He'd seen this chocolate-colored bear before . . . relief ripped through his veins. This mellow alpha was Tim's friend.

"Mr. Chocolate," he whispered.

Did the bear recognize its name? Mr. Chocolate blinked at Cody, then turned and ambled back the way he'd come. Back toward the upper lake.

Cody retrieved the rifle and followed. The massive alpha didn't seem to mind. Filled with gratitude for this friendly escort, he stayed close to the broad back as it led the way through the gloomy tunnel.

Mr. Chocolate was saving him.

Mr. Chocolate was helping him.

No!

Mr. Chocolate was veering off the trail.

"Hey, Mr. Chocolate. Just a little further," he begged in a

sing-song voice. "Just get me through the maze. Only a half mile more. Please!"

The grizzly looked back at him. Calm. Unfazed. Mr. Chocolate had other things to do. With a big paw, the bear uprooted a clump of soil and began scooping up bugs.

Feeling terribly alone, Cody kept moving.

In the sky, the buzzing floatplane began its descent.

A new fear spurred him forward. What if the pilot saw the damaged tents and decided it was too dangerous to get out of the plane? What if he took off after a few seconds of landing?

Cody threw all caution to the wind.

He sprinted like a linebacker, knowing every predator around would hear his footsteps but also knowing the end zone was in sight.

Almost there.

Fifty feet away, the arch ended. Long grass waved in the stormy breeze beyond. He leaped out into the open. It was a short dash, and then he was there, right on the upper lake's shore.

In the distance, the floatplane bobbed in the shallows. It was toy-sized from here.

Where was the pilot?

He wished he'd brought his binoculars.

He squinted at the knoll and Tim's campsite. A man with buzz-cut hair and broad shoulders stepped out of the trees. He strolled curiously toward the mashed tents. The pilot. He had no idea what danger he was in.

The man stopped and stared at the ruined tents, arms crossed. After a moment, he knelt and lifted the canvas. Then he reeled back and began hiking fast down the trail back to the lake. The pilot raised one hand to shield his eyes and nervously scanned the brush.

Cody was about to shout, to try and scream for the pilot not to leave, that he was here with his cousins, that they desperately needed a ride out, when he saw the bear.

Demon.

The killer grizzly. Moving on silent paws, the predator stalked the pilot. Twenty feet away and closing in fast. It would be on the pilot in seconds.

"Grizzly!" Cody screamed. "Behind you! Watch out!"

The pilot stopped in his tracks. "What's that?" he called. "What did you say? Treadwell, is that you?"

The pilot was completely oblivious.

Demon was just three body lengths behind him.

Cody gritted his teeth, raised the rifle, and fired into the air.

The pilot whirled around in shock. Seeing the grizzly, he took off fast, sprinting into the water. He scrambled onto the floats and into the cockpit and slammed the door. The grizzly skidded to a stop. Eyes fixed on the pilot, it paced the water's edge, huffing and snorting.

Ice cold sweat covered Cody. The bear looked like it was planning how to add the pilot to its food buffet.

"Hey kid!" the pilot yelled, finally catching sight of Cody. "Get away from here. That grizzly's dangerous. I'm calling the rangers for backup."

Did he think it was the only dangerous grizzly around?

Where did he want Cody to go?

"We're stranded. We need a ride back!"

The pilot stuck his head out the window. "What? Hold on!" He turned away and spoke into what looked like a radio or sat phone.

Cody had to get closer. He scrambled along the shore toward the river shouting, "We're stranded. Do you hear me? My cousins, they're down at the lower lake!"

He could see the pilot clearly through the windshield now, talking frantically and gesturing with his free hand.

Wait, where had Demon gone?

A massive splashing sound made every hair on Cody's neck stand on end. The grizzly was behind him. He'd forgotten bears can run thirty-five miles an hour. Cody turned as Demon reared up to its full height and roared.

The pilot leaned out the window and screamed, "Run!"

There was no way he could outrun it—grizzlies ran faster than Olympic sprinters.

Still, he could try.

Feet thudding, arms pumping, he ran for the alders. He was smaller. He could weave faster through the twisting trees. Mud sucked his boots. Brambles snagged his windbreaker and jeans. If only he could get a chance, a moment's breather, he'd fire the rifle.

But Demon was too close. He could almost feel its hot breath on his neck.

Suddenly, the alders thinned. Oh yikes, he was finished. Panic rose, sick in his throat. He pictured the claws sinking into his neck. His heart banged like a heavy metal drum.

Ahead lay a rocky outcrop. He'd climb up and make a stand. Just one good shot with the rifle could do it.

Boots sliding on the shale, he scrambled halfway up. The grizzly launched after him, its claws sending stones flying.

Trembling, Cody raised the rifle. Ready. Aim. Fire.

Bang.

Birds fluttered out of the brush. A creature screeched.

But he'd missed.

The grizzly roared. A bloodcurdling roar. Now the animal wasn't just after a meal. It was mad. It came leaping up the rocks. Demon would tear him to pieces.

Cody bounded the last few yards, moving like a mountain goat, his knee screaming in protest. Heaving for breath, he reached the top of the ridge. Below, white water cascaded into a pool. Was the creek deep enough to jump, or would he hit a rock?

The killer grizzly was mere feet away.

A wave of panic engulfed him.

Do something or die.

Cody flung his baseball cap at the bear. The grizzly lunged for it. That worked! Time to bolt.

Cody whirled around. Teetered at the edge of the ridge.

No! Not again. He struggled to keep his balance. With a sickening feeling, he realized he couldn't.

Down he went.

Down. Down. Down . . .

TWENTY

KATMAI NATIONAL PARK

Instinctively, Cody forced his limbs into place—legs straight, arms across his chest—just like he'd in an action movie.

He hit the water hard. Ice cold enveloped him. The shock made his whole body go stiff. He couldn't move, couldn't swim. The current shot him to the surface, and he gasped for air.

"Move," he shouted at his body through chattering teeth.

Painfully, his limbs struggling like dead weights, he managed to kick his head higher out of the surging stream.

The creek was moving fast. His boots weighed down his feet, and his jeans and waterproof jacket flapped awkwardly. His blood was turning to ice. He kicked again, harder this time.

Keep moving toward shore, keep moving and you'll stay warmer, have to get out!

The current dragged him tumbling down the creek, past rocks and fallen branches. He tried to aim for the bank.

To his horror, Demon was still tracking him.

Holy moly! No!

The grizzly loped along, jaws open like it was grinning. Like it knew where to nab its prey. It wasn't climbing into the river, though. The water must be too rough.

Cody looked around wildly. The current was depositing silt and branches on the opposite bank. That's where he needed to go. It was clear the grizzly couldn't cross over.

Pure adrenaline took over. He swam as he'd never swum in his life.

Almost there . . . shallow now . . .

Grunting, he grabbed a branch and pulled himself out. On his hands and knees, he crawled onto the muddy shore.

He lay, half-stunned and frozen.

"I win," he muttered through numb lips. "I win, Demon! Hear that? This win's for Treadwell."

He flopped back, breathing hard.

From the far bank, Cody heard a loud roar. When he finally found the energy to sit up again, the bear was gone.

Overhead, a second plane appeared. It circled, descending. He glimpsed the Alaska State Troopers insignia. Thank goodness. It would all be over soon.

He opened and closed his empty hands. Where was his rifle? He'd lost it when he fell.

Shaking with cold, he stumbled to his feet. Following the creek should lead him to the lower lake, to Samantha and Matt.

He staggered along, feeling like he was in the twilight zone. In a daze, he wandered until the river poured into the larger body of water.

His heart leaped when he spotted Matt's small blue tent.

"Samantha! Matt!" he shouted.

No answer.

"Samantha!"

Panting, he reached the tent. Empty.

A seagull screeched and wheeled.

What now?

And then he let out a deep breath of relief when he saw them running through the seagrass.

"Samantha!" he yelled.

She raced up and threw her arms around him. "I was worried. You were gone for ages. What happened with the plane? We saw it land. And another just flew over."

Matt scowled. "Yeah, you took long enough. What the heck! What's happened to our ride out? You should've got the pilot to fly here!"

Samantha held Cody by the shoulder as if only now realizing he was drenched and half frozen to death.

"Are you alright?" she demanded. "What happened?"

"Demon's on the hunt."

Matt wrinkled his nose. "Demon? What, is that some kind of joke?"

"It's a grizzly," Samantha said.

Cody cut in. "Quick. We need to start a fire. The biggest fire we can make. It might not just be Demon on the hunt. Something set the grizzlies off. Hurry!"

Matt started moaning but Samantha screamed, "Be quiet and do what Cody says. Right now, Matt!"

Startled, he scowled at her. Then he actually stomped around gathering wood.

Cody said, "We need to keep the bears away. And we

need to make the biggest signal fire we can. I want to make sure those rangers find us."

"Does the pilot know we're here?" Samantha said, arranging kindling on the beach.

"He knows Demon went after me. They'll be looking for us, I guarantee it."

She nodded. "So, you made it to the upper lake. Great job. You can tell me what happened later. Let's get this fire going."

TWENTY-ONE

Katmai National Park

Cody, Samantha, and Matt built the blaze until it roared ten feet high. The heat felt fantastic. That and a sleeping bag around Cody's shoulders stripped the cold from his quaking limbs.

He sighed in relief as the Coast Guard plane came in for a perfect landing and taxied to the shore.

A wiry, red-haired trooper opened the door and leaned out. "Great job with the signal fire. Made our job finding you a whole lot easier."

The cousins hauled their stuff toward the plane. Even though much of their gear was ruined, they knew to respect the land. This was grizzly territory—and fox, wolf, moose, rabbit, and all the other animals that called this place home.

Leave nothing behind except your footprints.

Well, the axe was somewhere in the woods and the gun, too, but Cody and Samantha had done what they could.

While the trooper stowed their gear, the pilot gave them a hand up. "What are you kids doing here?"

"It's a long story," Cody said.

"I'm sure it is."

Cody squashed into a seat beside Samantha. Matt fell into the aisle seat. A second trooper, this one older and bearded, handed Samantha a blanket and a thermos.

She filled cups with hot coffee and passed them around. Cody gulped his share. It was sweet with lots of milk, and he decided it was the most delicious thing he'd ever tasted.

When the cup was empty, he wiped his mouth on his sleeve and asked the question he'd been dreading. But he had to know.

"Sir?" he said,

The red-haired trooper met his eyes.

"Did you find Tim Treadwell and Amie?"

The trooper watched him for a long moment and then turned to the window, gazing out. "I'm sorry, son. We did. They didn't make it."

The pilot pulled back the yoke, and the floatplane rose into the air.

Hot tears filled Cody's eyes. He pressed his face to the window and watched the dark grizzly maze spread out below. In the creeks, a few bears were still catching salmon as if nothing had happened.

Tim Treadwell, the incredible bear expert. And Amie, his friend and companion in this wild place. They were gone.

The troopers talked in low voices. Cody strained to hear.

"I thought I'd have a heart attack when that grizzly charged," the older man said. "That animal had no fear. Even against four of us."

"Yeah. And that second grizzly?" the red-haired trooper said. "I thought he'd get me for sure. He was just as aggressive."

Cody flashed a glance at Samantha. Quietly, he said, "Demon and Machine?"

"Sounds like it," she whispered. "Or some other starving bears."

The older trooper shook his head. "Terrible scene. But Treadwell shouldn't have been in the park, what with the drought and all. At this time of year? No one should be up here." He gave Cody, Samantha, and Matt a sharp look.

Cody stared at his feet. The trooper was right.

The plane's engine rumbled like a flying lawnmower as they soared over the dark ocean.

With an electronic squawk, the radio stuttered to life. The pilot turned up the volume:

Bodies presumed to be Timothy Treadwell and his companion. Park rangers will be returning to the site tomorrow.

The news had already caught wind of the story. Word traveled fast.

Cody's heart ached. There'd been something beautiful about Tim's love for the bears. He thought about Mr. Chocolate, the gentle bear who'd escorted him through the maze. Of the injured bear and the mother grizzly with her cubs. Miraculous as it seemed, Tim and many of the bears had formed a bond, anyone could see that.

Grizzlies were incredible animals, born to live in this wilderness.

If only Tim and Amie had taken the earlier flight home to California. Then the last few days would never have happened.

Samantha spoke up. "What I don't understand is why—after all this time Tim was up here—why would a grizzly suddenly attack him like that?"

"Who knows. Hunger? Aggression?"

Matt sneered. "Because they're killers, that's why."

"Truth is, most bears wouldn't kill a man," the older trooper said. "They're more interested in fish and other prey. But sometimes you get what they call the twenty-fifth grizzly—the bear that mauls and kills."

Cody nodded. He understood completely. For where there had been gentleness in Mr. Chocolate's eyes, in Demon's, there had been only rage. Just like people, bears came in all sorts.

Matt said, "Can't you fly this thing any faster? I thought you guys were the Coast Guard. How much longer? I need a beer."

Samantha planted her face in her hands and sighed with embarrassment. Cody groaned.

Some people never changed.

TWENTY-TWO

KODIAK ISLAND, ALASKA

At Kodiak Airport, Gramps met the plane. He hugged Cody, Matt, and Samantha, pulling them one-by-one into his bomber-jacket-clad chest.

Cody inhaled the familiar smell. Gramps smelled like a pipe and soap and felt as warm and solid as ever.

Gramps didn't say a word about what they'd done. When they got to the cabin, he made hot dogs on a big grill.

Cody scoffed down three, smothered with mustard, fried tomato, and onions. He burped. "That was great, thanks."

"You guys will make me old before my time." Gramps stared into the glowing coals. "It's tragic what happened to Tim Treadwell. He was a goofy type of guy, but I liked him. A local was talking stink about him at the airport, saying he asked for it."

"That's unfair!" Cody said. "All he was doing was trying to protect bears from poachers."

Gramps nodded. "Yeah. But he took his chances. Grizzlies are wild animals."

"Was it just bad luck?" Cody asked, trying to come to terms with what had happened.

"I don't know, son," Gramps scratched his salt-and-pepper beard. "If you play with fire, one day you'll get burned. Treadwell ditched the bear spray and an electric fence. Still, he managed to survive thirteen summers in bear central. Not many could do that."

"I know we should never have gone to the grizzly maze, Cody said.

His grandfather raised his eyebrows. "You've got that right. That was one of the scariest moments of my life—when the Park rangers called and told me the three of you were in the maze. I thought you were at the Best Western in Kodiak."

"I'm sorry," Samantha said, her face flushed.

"I dashed down to the park ranger's office," Gramps said. "A ranger broke it to me that Treadwell had disappeared. He said you three were in the grizzly maze and that there was a killer bear on the prowl." Gramps cleared his throat. "Yep. I nearly had a heart attack."

Cody felt his face grow hot.

"Your parents called," Gramps said. "They want you home immediately—sooner if possible." He cleared his throat. "Guess this is the last time they trust you with me."

"It never would have happened if Cody hadn't bought those tickets with his dad's credit card," Matt muttered.

Cody leaped to his feet. "Lying jerk!"

"Cool it, guys." Gramps grabbed Cody's arm. "Thank goodness you're okay."

"Sorry, Gramps," Cody said.

"I know you're sorry, son." Gramps wrapped one arm around Cody's shoulders. "How about a four-way cuddle. Remember how we used to do this when you were little?"

"I'm not a big cuddler," Matt muttered.

"Aw! Come on, son."

Scowling, Matt joined them.

Cody hugged his grandfather and Samantha. Then he forced himself to hug Matt too, although he didn't feel like it. Matt was a jerk, but he was family.

After a moment, Matt returned his hug.

Cody stifled a surprised gasp.

Gramps brought out marshmallows, and they gathered closer to the fire to make s'mores.

"I love your place here." Cody looked up at the dark firs and the snow-covered mountains. "I want to come back to Alaska. Do you think being an Alaskan park ranger would be a good career?"

Gramps scratched his beard. "Certainly an interesting

one. I admire the park rangers—they're a brave bunch."

"I could go to college in Anchorage," Cody said.

Gramps smiled. "That would be good. I'd see a lot more of you then."

Cody grinned. Despite what happened, he loved the wilderness. And he admired Tim Treadwell for trying to protect wild animals. He also admired the rangers and state troopers. They protected wild animals too. His heart stirred at the possibility of joining them one day.

He mashed a hot marshmallow and a chocolate square between two graham crackers and popped it into his mouth. "I can't believe we did that, wandered all over grizzly territory right before hibernation season."

"We had no idea what we were getting into," Samantha agreed.

"Nope. That place belongs to the bears. We were lucky, very lucky. But we did it," Cody said, looking at his cousins. "I don't know how, but we survived. The three of us. We escaped the grizzly maze!"

THE END

Turn the page for amazing facts about grizzlies and more!

10 TIPS TO SURVIVE A GRIZZLY ATTACK

1. Don't run. Stand your ground and slowly wave your arms up and down to look bigger. Pick up small children and warn them to be quiet.
2. Avoid eye contact; move away quietly, slowly and sideways so as not to trip. Do not scream—that will accelerate the situation.
3. Get to a safe place like a car or a building. Know that grizzlies can climb trees.
4. Throw a hat or your jacket to distract the bear.
5. Ask rangers about bear sightings and areas to avoid.
6. Carry bear spray and read how to use it. Keep it within reach, and practice pulling it out fast.
7. If the bear attacks, use whatever you have to hit the bear in the face or muzzle.
8. Never approach any bear, especially a mother bear with cubs.
9. If a bear attacks your tent, do not play dead. It's looking for food and sees you as prey. Keep bear spray, a flashlight, or an air horn handy—you may have only minutes to find them in the dark.
10. Never eat or keep food in your tent. Store food in bear-tight containers away from the tent. Do not leave garbage around.

DID YOU KNOW?

AMAZING GRIZZLY FACTS

Despite their ferocious reputations, up to 80% of a grizzly bear's diet consists of insects, grass, berries, roots, and broad-leaved plants. The other 20% consists of meat and fish, such as rodents, wolves, elk, moose, clams, salmon, and even the occasional whale carcass.

Grizzlies have an excellent sense of smell. They can smell an open peanut butter jar from two miles away. They can also smell clams through the sand, which helps them dig them up.

A grizzly standing on its hind legs is tall enough to look through a second-story window.

Grizzles can run at speeds of 35 miles per hour.

A grizzly is so strong that it can kill a wolf with one swipe of its massive paw.

The big hump on a grizzly's back is made of muscle,

giving the bear its mighty strength. In fact, they have the strongest front limbs of any animal in the world.

Bears love honey. Their furry, thick skin protects them from bee stings when they pull apart a bee hive.

The grizzlies in Katmai National Park are among the largest bears in the world. They live longer than bears in regions where hunting is allowed and grow up to 1,400 pounds.

Grizzlies rarely kill people. About eighty percent of those attacks are by mother bears defending their cubs or bears defending their food cache. Predatory attacks are rare. However, they do happen.

Grizzly bears have been a threatened species since 1975.

The State of Alaska has around 32,000 bears and only 670,000 people. That's one bear for every 21 people!

Participate in Fat Bear Week!

Do you love bears? Participate in Katmai National Park's Fat Bear Week! It's an annual tradition. Every fall, internet users watch live bear cams and vote for their favorite fat bear.

Learn more at: https://explore.org/fat-bear-week

WHO WAS TIMOTHY TREADWELL?

Timothy Treadwell was a Californian wildlife activist with the unusual ability to communicate with the largest omnivores on the planet. Treadwell loved grizzly bears and wanted to protect them from both illegal poachers and sports hunters. He also wished to convince everyone that they're not the ferocious predators they seem.

Treadwell spent thirteen summers living closely with grizzlies in Alaska. In winter, Treadwell returned to California to campaign passionately for the bears. He wanted to be part of their lives and to educate young people about them.

He documented his experiences in writing and videos. Treadwell wrote a touching and fascinating book called *Among Grizzlies: Living with Wild Bears in Alaska.*

He also formed an educational, non-profit company called *Grizzly People.*

The last thing Treadwell would have wanted was to become known as Katmai National Park's first grizzly fatality.

Park Rangers and other bear researchers repeatedly warned Treadwell that getting close to grizzlies was dangerous. Treadwell was aware of the danger.

In interviews, he warned:

"Do not do this. Do not copy me."

He said that if a bear killed him, he didn't want the bear to be blamed:

"If they ever come to pick me up and find me dead, I hope they just bury me and don't say a word."

Treadwell had not planned to be in the park in October 2003. He tried to fly back to California but argued with the airline ticketer over the high ticket price. He decided to wait until the prices came down and returned to the park.

On October 5, he talked to a friend via satellite phone and mentioned no problems with the bears. The following day, however, a Kodiak air taxi pilot found their campsite deserted, apart from a massive bear. The pilot contacted park rangers, who quickly determined that Timothy Treadwell and Amie Huguenard had not survived.

A film, *Grizzly Man* (2005), documents Treadwell's life and was aired on the Discovery Channel. *The Grizzly Man Diaries* (2008) is an 8-episode miniseries that premiered on Animal Planet and also documents Treadwell's work and life using interviews and historical footage.

While people disagree over whether Timothy Treadwell was right or wrong to live so close to grizzlies, his work has given us a fascinating and unique understanding of grizzlies and their habitats.

FASCINATING QUOTES

"I felt a great deal of paranoia, and rightfully so… A nearby creek was loaded with bears and trouble. The chemistry between the bears was volatile—three mean bears . . . I felt the tension growing."
Timothy Treadwell, August 21.

"But, let me tell you, … every fish, every bear was here. We made the best friggin' choice of our lives. Once the rain settled down, boy, it was amazing out here."
Timothy Treadwell, two days before his death.

"Bears wishing to traverse the area would have had to either wade in the lake or walk right next to the tent. A person could not have designed a more dangerous location to set up a camp…His decision not to have any defensive methods or bear deterrents in the camp was directly responsible for the catastrophic event."
Larry Van Daele, Biologist.

"If it happens, it happens. God forbid, if a bear takes me, let him go."
Timothy Treadwell.

"We are deeply saddened by the loss of our friend and admired environmental warrior."

Pierre Brosnan, actor, after learning of Treadwell's death.

"At the top of the food chain, the magnificent grizzly bear has no animal to fear but the two-legged kind. Two hundred years ago, Europeans settled in the best habitat and killed thousands of grizzly bears, which they saw as competition or a threat. Grizzly bear numbers plummeted in the lower 48 states, reduced to just 1% of their former numbers and relegated to the most remote remaining wilderness areas.

Grizzly People Pamphlet.

"I had a lot of special guests come in. Timothy was always the one they'd remember. He was always the favorite. In part, it was the bears, but it was really his personal style…He was like a little kid, almost like a jumping bean. He had so much energy. This was his passion. His love. He was so honest, and the kids identified with that.

Valerie Roach, 3rd-Grade Teacher, California

"I admired how serious Timothy's messages were. He risks his life for the bears."

Californian School Student

"Watching him perform in a classroom, you saw a magician who explained the mysteries of bears and their lives in such a way that children emerged glowing as if they too were the discoverers of wild

America. Hearing him talk about his bears, by name, with their bonds of affection, quirky behavior, and playful antics, you felt that you were let in on great secrets that few receive today or have forgotten as wilderness has been paved over and subdivided."

Louisa Willcox, Director, Natural Resources Defense Council.

THE I ESCAPED SERIES

I Escaped North Korea!

I Escaped The California Camp Fire

I Escaped The World's Deadliest Shark Attack

I Escaped Amazon River Pirates

I Escaped The Donner Party

I Escaped The Salem Witch Trials

I Escaped Pirates In The Caribbean

I Escaped The Tower of London

I Escaped Egypt's Deadliest Train Disaster

I Escaped The Haunted Winchester House

I Escaped The Gold Rush Fever

I Escaped The Prison Island

I Escaped The Grizzly Maze

More great adventures coming soon!

JOIN THE I ESCAPED CLUB

Get a free pack of mazes and word finds to print and play!

https://www.subscribepage.com/escapedclub

BIBLIOGRAPHY

Jans, Nick, *The Grizzly Maze, Timothy Treadwell's Fatal Obsession with Alaskan Bears,* Dutton, Jan 2005.

Herzog, Werner, *Grizzly Man,* documentary film, 2005

Treadwell, Timothy, *Among Grizzlies, Living with Wild Bears in Alaska,* Feb, 1999

https://www.yellowstone-bearman.com/Tim_Treadwell.html, *Night of the Grizzly,* 2005

NPS Report Treadwell Grizzly Fatality, Nov, 20, 2003, Dalrymple, Derek. Katmai Park Ranger. 2003 National Park Service Incident Report, pages 11, 12.

Ellis, Joel. Katmai National Park Ranger. 2003 Scene Investigator. 2003 Park Service Incident Report; pages 1-9